He couldn't let her go....

Not until her would-be killer was behind bars. Only, if Eve had made up her mind to go back, how in the devil was he supposed to stop her? Kidnap her himself?

Maybe that wasn't such a bad idea.

He studied her across the table. The dark circles around her eyes, the stoop of her shoulders revealed that the growing threat of danger was weighing on her.

And still he ached to just carry her off somewhere and...

And what? Finish what he'd started last night? Kiss her senseless? Make love to her?

All of the above, he admitted.

He was falling for Eve. Hard.

The realization galloped through him and he felt like a spooked stallion. More than the approaching killer, that frightened the hell out of him.

JOANNA WAYNE

GENUINE COWBOY

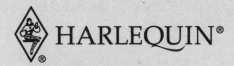

TORONTO • NEW YORK • LONDON
AMSTERDAM • PARIS • SYDNEY • HAMBURG
STOCKHOLM • ATHENS • TOKYO • MILAN • MADRID
PRAGUE • WARSAW • BUDAPEST • AUCKLAND

To my good friends Patsy and Hill,
who are always there when I need them for golf, fun or
just to talk. They are part of the reason I LOVE living in Texas.
And to my marvelous editor, who keeps me on track.

Recycling programs
for this product may
not exist in your area.

ISBN-13: 978-0-373-74570-8

GENUINE COWBOY

Copyright © 2010 by Jo Ann Vest

www.eHarlequin.com

Printed in U.S.A.

ABOUT THE AUTHOR

Joanna Wayne was born and raised in Shreveport, Louisiana, and received her undergraduate and graduate degrees from LSU-Shreveport. She moved to New Orleans in 1984, and it was there that she attended her first writing class and joined her first professional writing organization. Her debut novel, *Deep in the Bayou*, was published in 1994.

Now, dozens of published books later, Joanna has made a name for herself as being on the cutting edge of romantic suspense in both series and single-title novels. She has been on the Waldenbooks bestseller list for romance and has won many industry awards. She is also a popular speaker at writing organizations and local community functions and has taught creative writing at the University of New Orleans Metropolitan College.

Joanna currently resides in a small community forty miles north of Houston, Texas, with her husband. Though she still has many family and emotional ties to Louisiana, she loves living in the Lone Star State. You may write Joanna at P.O. Box 852, Montgomery, Texas 77356.

Books by Joanna Wayne

HARLEQUIN INTRIGUE

1001—24 KARAT AMMUNITION*
1019—TEXAS GUN SMOKE*
1041—POINT BLANK PROTECTOR*
1065—LOADED*
1096—MIRACLE AT COLTS RUN CROSS*
1123—COWBOY COMMANDO†
1152—COWBOY TO THE CORE†
1167—BRAVO, TANGO, COWBOY†

1195—COWBOY DELIRIUM*†
1228—COWBOY SWAGGER**
1249—GENUINE COWBOY**

*Four Brothers of Colts Run Cross
†Special Ops Texas
**Sons of Troy Ledger

CAST OF CHARACTERS

Sean Ledger—Horse trainer with a reputation for being a whisperer. A son of Troy Ledger.

Eve Worthington—Single mother and the former psychiatrist to Troy Ledger.

Joey Worthington—Eve's five-year-old son.

Troy Ledger—Convicted of killing his wife eighteen years ago. Released from prison on a technicality, he is obsessed with finding his late wife's killer.

Dylan Ledger—Sean's brother who has recently settled on Willow Creek Ranch.

Collette Ledger—Dylan's wife. She is convinced of Troy's innocence.

Wyatt Ledger—Sean's older brother, currently a homicide detective in Atlanta.

Orson Bastion—Escaped convict out for revenge.

Gordon Epps—Troy's prison warden when he was in prison.

Alyssa Coleman—Orson's sister.

Nick Coleman—Alyssa's son.

Detective Reagan Conner—Out to arrest Orson Bastion and return him to prison at any cost.

Chapter One

"Mommy! Mommy! Don't let him get me!"

Eve Worthington jerked awake at the sound of her young son's voice and then dodged the agile body that propelled itself from the floor into the middle of her bed.

She gathered Joey into her arms. "Did you have a nightmare, sweetie?"

"A man was in my room. He was going to hurt me."

"It's okay, Joey. There's no one in the house but you and me. You're safe. I won't let anyone hurt you."

She kissed the top of Joey's head and let her lips linger in the soft blond hair that smelled like sunshine and springtime. She held him close, her hands splayed across his back until the shudders stopped.

It had been two years since he'd lost his father to a drive-by shooting mere blocks from their Dallas home. He'd been almost four years old at the time, independent and curious, a ball of energy who was eager for any adventure.

Now he seldom made it through the night without waking screaming, in the throes of a nightmare. He held tightly on to her hand whenever the two of them left the house. Even at the neighborhood park that he loved, he didn't want her out of his sight, especially if there was a man around. When she'd tried to enroll him in kindergarten, he'd become so distraught, she'd decided to hold him back a year.

She was a psychiatrist. She should know how to help Joey get past this, know how to make him feel safe. Her mentor and favorite professor, Edgar Callen, claimed she was simply too close to the situation to be objective.

Edgar was probably right but her own fears went much deeper than even he knew. Her three years of working with prisoners in Texas correctional institutions had left their scars even before she'd lost her husband.

Her friend Miriam, whom she seldom saw anymore, also a psychiatrist, believed that Eve had become far too protective of Joey.

Miriam was likely correct in her assessment as well. But Joey had been through so much that Eve couldn't help being overly cautious with him.

"Can I sleep with you, Mommy?"

"You'll be more comfortable in your bed. I'll come and lie down with you until you fall asleep."

"I don't want to go back in there."

"We'll turn on all the lights and look around. When you see your toys and stuffed animals, you'll know the bad dream wasn't real."

"It seemed real."

"I know it did. Nightmares are like that, but there's nothing in your room when the light is off that's not there when the light is on."

She scooted to the edge of the bed, then threw her bare feet to the floor, just as a streak of lightning zigzagged across the night sky. Joey stood on the mattress and wrapped his short arms around her neck.

She picked him up, noting, as always, how light he felt in her arms. He was small for his age and a difficult eater, constantly complaining of stomach pains. The pediatrician had ruled out any medical reasons for them.

Once back in his room, they spent a good

half hour making sure every toy was in place. By the time he'd settled in his bed with his stuffed lion, a light rain was slapping against the window and low rumbles of thunder growled in the distance.

Eve snuggled beside her son until he fell asleep, though she doubted he'd sleep soundly with the storm kicking up outside. There was little use to go back to her room only to be dragged from bed again.

She climbed out of his bed stealthily and turned down the quilt on the spare twin bed in Joey's room. Finally, Eve drifted into a sound sleep. When she opened her eyes again, it was half-past six. Amazingly, both she and Joey had slept through the rest of the night.

She stretched and turned to check on her son. He'd kicked off his covers, but his lion was still clutched tightly to his chest. She listened to his gentle breathing, watched the steady rise and fall of his chest and felt a tightening in her throat.

Moving quietly so as not to wake him, she climbed from the bed and walked to the bedroom door, lingering to look back at Joey. If only he always looked as peaceful as he did this minute.

Padding to the rear of the house, she started

a pot of coffee, pausing when she was done to stare out the kitchen window. The thunderstorm had given way to a calm dawn, but water puddled the lawn and dripped from the few leaves that clung stubbornly to the lone oak tree.

Eve went back to her bedroom for her slippers before walking almost to the street to retrieve the plastic-wrapped copy of *The Dallas Morning News.* When she'd worked, reading the newspaper had been a luxury reserved for weekends and holidays. Now that she'd become a full-time mother to her troubled son, it was part of her morning routine.

Stripping away the wet wrapper, she tossed it into the trash and spread the paper on the kitchen table as the odor of fresh-perked coffee filled the room. The headlines dealt with the wrangling between local politicians. She ignored it and skimmed the rest of the page before flipping to an inside section.

Her breath caught as her focus centered on a black-and-white photograph at the top of the page. The caption beneath the picture gave her chills.

Orson Bastion had escaped from the Texas State Penitentiary at Huntsville, Texas.

Eve sank into the chair as her mind dragged

her into the past. Her home phone rang, startling her back into the present. She checked the caller ID. Gordon Epps, the prison's warden. She lifted the receiver.

"I just read about Orson's escape," she said, saving him the trouble of trying to break it to her gently.

"I was afraid of that. Are you okay?"

"I've had better mornings. When did he escape?"

"Sometime during the night. He was first missed at the 2:00 a.m. security check. One of the security patrol found the guard pulling night duty on Orson's wing dead. He'd been strangled."

"Orson's calling card. Are you sure he escaped the premises?"

"Relatively sure. We've spent the night searching and there's no sign of him. Speculation is that he somehow rode out with the trash."

At least he was with his own kind.

"He took the guard's gun, so we know he's armed."

"And there's no doubt he's dangerous," Eve added. "He could be anywhere by now."

"Law enforcement officers across the state have been notified. With any luck, he'll be back in custody in a matter of hours. Still, I wanted to give you a heads-up."

"You don't think he'll come after me, do you? I haven't had any dealings with him in two years. He must have a lot worse enemies than me to get even with."

"I suspect Orson's only interested in saving his own hide now. He's likely keeping a low profile and hightailing it out of the state as fast as he can."

"I hope you're right."

"If you're worried at all, Eve, you could always go spend a few days with Troy Ledger. His ranch is not that far away, and I know he'd love to see you."

"How is he?"

"Adjusting well to freedom. He's reunited with his son Dylan and they're working his old ranch."

"Then I doubt he'd be thrilled about my running to him at the first sign of trouble."

"Just a thought. How's the boy?" Epps asked.

"Joey's making progress, but still experiencing a lot of anxiety and separation issues."

"I hate to hear that. I've got to run, Eve, but if there's anything I can do, give me a call. And think about paying a visit to Troy.

If Orson is stupid enough to seek revenge against you for your testimony at his parole hearing, he'd never think of looking for you at the home of a former inmate accused of killing his own wife."

If Orson was stupid enough to come after her... But Orson wasn't stupid. She'd seen the results of his intelligence testing. He bordered on genius. That didn't mean he wasn't evil to the core. And he *had* threatened to get back at her for fouling his early parole attempt.

Orson's threat echoed in her mind. She had no doubt when he'd hurled it at her that he'd meant every word. So how could she convince herself that he wouldn't come after her now?

"I appreciate the call, Gordon."

"Okay, and keep me posted if you decide to leave home. If you stay, you need to alert the police that Orson could show up there. Demand protection. Promise me you'll do that."

"I'm not sure the Dallas Police Department responds to citizen demands."

"Then go see Troy for a few days. He'll understand and you're surely not afraid of him. You've said yourself that you'd never met a prisoner whose innocence was as compelling as Troy's."

She had been convinced of his innocence, had even made a statement to the press on his release that she'd trust him with her life and the life of her son.

She'd meant the words at the time. But was she ready to put them to the test?

Did she dare not?

Chapter Two

The frosty late November air had a bite to it, and the wind stung Sean Ledger's face as he ducked through the door and into the cozy barn. He was up early and raring to go to work. He had a feeling this just might be the day he made some real headway with Go Lightly.

He'd been at Cahill Horse Farm for just over six months and Go Lightly was still a challenge. The horse had racing in its blood and was fast enough to be a threat in any of the major races for two-year-olds.

Until the starter fired his shot and the gates opened. Then Go Lightly bucked and fought the jockey, as if he were being asked to run along a track planted with land mines. Ted Cahill was about ready to give up on the animal. Sean wasn't.

He just needed more time, and fewer distractions—compliments of Tom's wife.

Women. Sean didn't understand them and doubted he ever would. Give him a horse any day. Sean could get into a horse's mind, figure out what had frightened it or killed its spirit. Given time, Scan could usually bring a horse around.

Women, on the other hand, were beyond comprehension. As far as he was concerned, they weren't just from another planet, but from another galaxy. And they were welcome to it.

He pushed the irritating thoughts aside and tuned into the life pulsing in the barn. Suzy pawed at the pile of hay at her feet, threw back her head and snorted.

"Good morning, old girl." Sean reached over and scratched the long nose. "You don't like being ignored, do you?"

Suzy snorted again and stretched her head over the stall door so that she could rub against the rough denim of Sean's jacket.

Thunder threw back his head and neighed loudly, then kicked his back feet, protesting any- and everything. Aptly named, he was the most high spirited of all the quarter horses at Cahill Farms. He'd been a winner in his day, and he knew it. The past glory earned him the right to be a contrary sire.

The stud settled a bit, almost gloatingly, when Sean turned his attention to him. Sean shrugged out of his denim jacket and hung it on a peg near the door. Leaning against a support post, he pulled a folded envelope from his shirt pocket. He removed the letter, the latest from his brother Dylan. After reading through it, Sean reread the last paragraph.

"You'd love the Texas Hill Country, Sean. Pay us a visit, if only for a few days. Give Dad a chance. You won't be sorry."

Troy did not share Dylan's confidence that he'd like returning to the ranch. And as for giving Troy Ledger a chance, those days were long gone. When he was a kid, he'd had his father on a pedestal so high the man would have needed a parachute to come back to earth safely.

Troy Ledger hadn't utilized a parachute or a safety net. He'd nosedived off the perch into the pool of blood that had soaked Sean's brutally slain mother.

"Is that a love letter?"

Sean turned at the seductive voice, nodded to Sasha Cahill, then folded the letter and stuffed it back in his pocket. "Far from it."

"I'll bet you left lots of broken hearts back in Kentucky when you came to work for my father."

Not a subject he was interested in pursuing, especially not with his boss's seventeen- going on twenty-one-year-old daughter. "Don't you have school today?"

"Teacher Institute day. You don't mind my company, do you?"

"I'm paid to work, not socialize."

"I love watching you interact with Go Lightly. Your voice and the way you touch him makes me wish I was an emotionally scarred racehorse you were out to save."

Oh, good grief. It was bad enough that Sasha's mother came on to him like a dog in heat. Now Sasha. If it was something in the water, Ted Cahill had best dig his family a new well.

"You're not a horse." She was a spoiled brat, though he refrained from saying so. "Why don't you take Suzy out for a ride? She could use a good workout."

"Horses aren't the only animals that need a whisperer, Sean."

The whisperer label was one Sean had never encouraged. It sounded like magic and tended to make people expect miracles. Sean was not a magician. He walked away, heading toward the back of the horse barn where he had a small office.

"Please come riding with me, Sean. I hate to ride alone. You know Mom's worthless before noon and Daddy's gone for the day."

Her voice had that breathless quality that made her sound like a hormonally charged adolescent trying out for the role of Lolita. If he was her father, he'd ground her until she was past the pimple stage.

Sean shook his head. "Sorry, *kid,* I have work to do."

He strode past the horses, stepped into his office and closed the door behind him. Had there been a bolt, he'd have locked it. The idea of owning his own quarter horse farm sounded better by the day, and he probably had enough money saved to pull it off if he still took on a few private clients who owned problem horses.

He tossed his hat to the top of a stack of unopened cardboard boxes and plopped onto the worn chair behind the metal desk. Remembering the letter, he pulled it from his pocket and dropped it into the top drawer to be answered later—with a very succinct "no."

Forging a relationship with a father he hadn't seen since the day the man received a life sentence for murdering his mother didn't hold a lot of appeal for Sean. Release on a technicality didn't wash away the man's sins.

The door to Sean's office squeaked open. He groaned. When he finally looked up, Sasha's jacket was dangling from a crooked finger. Her chest was bare, her firm breasts pointing at him as if daring him to resist temptation.

He took a deep breath—and the dare. "Put your jacket on, Sasha. You're too smart, too pretty and way too young to be playing this stupid game. Don't devalue what you are inside by throwing yourself at me or anyone else."

She leaned against the rough-hewn doorframe. "Look at me, Sean. You'll see I'm old enough."

Sean stood and grabbed his Stetson. When he reached the door, he picked up Sasha at the waist to move her out of his way. The crazy kid threw her legs around him and pressed her bare breasts against his chest.

He heard footsteps and cringed as he looked up to find Laci Cahill staring at him. The old adage "If looks could kill" had never seemed more apt.

Laci propped her hands on her hips. "Well, this explains a lot."

"This is not what it looks like," he assured Sasha's mother.

Laci's irate glare made it clear that she didn't believe him.

Thankfully, Sasha had dismounted his hips at her mother's appearance and was pulling on her jacket at a speed that he'd previously only seen her exhibit when texting messages on her touch-screen cell phone.

Laci stepped inside the office. "Go to your room, Sasha."

Sasha scooted past him without a glance.

"Why bother with the old mare when you have the filly?" Laci snapped.

"I'm here to train horses, Laci. That's all, and I definitely didn't initiate that scene you just walked in on."

"Do you expect me to believe that?"

"I can't control what you believe, but I'm telling you the truth."

"Stay away from my daughter, Sean. If I ever catch the two of you in another compromising position, I'll not only see that Ted fires you, but that you never work as a trainer again. Do I make myself clear?"

"Crystal clear."

In fact, a lot of things were clear right now, mainly that he couldn't work in this type of strained environment. "I'll pack my things and be off the Cahill property by noon."

"What's that supposed to mean?"

"You don't have to worry about watching me every second or firing me. I quit."

Laci grabbed his arm. "That's not necessary. I know how Sasha is. This isn't the first time she's pulled something like this."

Talk about changing horses in midstream. A minute ago, Sean was to blame for everything. Now it was Sasha. A man could get dizzy trying to keep up.

"I'll leave Ted the names of a couple of guys he might want to interview for my job," Sean said. Older men who hopefully wouldn't be subjected to seduction at every turn. "And don't worry, I'll leave you and Sasha out of my explanation for leaving on such short notice."

"You're making a mistake, Sean. There's not a trainer in the state who wouldn't salivate at the thought of going to work for Ted Cahill."

"And now one lucky applicant will get to drool all over his work shirt." Sean tipped his hat and walked away. Amazing, how a man could start out a day with great expectations, only to have it blow up in his face.

Sean went back to the desk and pulled his brother's letter from the drawer. Dylan's written words weighed heavy on his mind as he retrieved his worn jacket and walked back to his small cabin to gather his things. Maybe a trip to the Texas Hill Country wasn't such a bad idea after all.

It would be good to see Dylan again and finally meet his brother's new wife—before Dylan's dreams of idyllic marriage evolved into reality.

Or maybe that kind of luckless romance was reserved for Sean.

Chapter Three

Troy Ledger turned off the TV and walked back to his small kitchen, taking his half-empty plate with him. He'd just caught the tail end of the six o'clock news, and that had been enough to kill his appetite.

Orson Bastion had escaped from the pen and taken out a guard in the process. Talk about a brutal reminder of his prison life. Impulsively, his hand moved to the scar on his cheek.

His thoughts moved to Eve Worthington. The news of Bastion's escape had to be frightening for her. If he had her phone number he'd call her. But best that he didn't have it. For all he knew, she'd left the area by now.

Troy washed his plate, rinsed it and stood it in the drainer. He reached for the skillet he'd used to fry a slice of ham for his sandwich and immersed it in the hot, soapy water. The old dishwasher needed replacing, but there wasn't much need for a fancy machine when a man lived alone.

His son, Dylan, and Dylan's new wife, Collette, had moved out of the old family house and into their starter ranch house two weeks earlier. They needed their privacy. They were only a good horse ride away, but Troy missed them a lot more than he was willing to admit.

Troy and Dylan had built the newlyweds' house themselves, with lots of suggestions from Collette. She was quite a woman, even reminded him of Helene a little. Not that he needed a reminder of Helene. She was seldom far from his mind and never out of his heart. Never had been. Never would be.

But the last few months of working with his son on the house and the ranch they were getting up and running again had meant more to Troy than Dylan could possibly realize. Seventeen years in prison had robbed Troy of much of his five sons' childhood and all of their adolescence. They'd grown from boys to men without him. Dylan was the only one of the five who'd shown any interest in having Troy back in his life. He prayed that would change one day, but he couldn't count on it.

Troy finished the dishes and dried his hands. It was only six in the evening, but he was exhausted. Working from sunup to sundown did that for a man. Fatigue didn't bother him. The prospect of spending another night alone in the rambling old house did.

He could handle the days, but alone at night, memories of Helene haunted his mind. He could hear her laughter, sweet and melodic, filling the house as she interacted with their rambunctious sons.

He could smell her fragrance, like a bouquet from the garden she'd pampered like one of their children. He could see her on Sunday morning, her dark, shiny hair dancing about her shoulders, leading them all to church whether they liked it or not.

But the most devastating memories came when he crawled into the bed he'd once shared with Helene. It had taken him weeks to even enter the master bedroom, had taken weeks more before he could bear sleeping in the bed.

Even now, three months later, he couldn't stretch out between the sheets without his arms literally aching to wrap around her and feel her warm, loving body cuddled against his. Some nights the pain was all but unbearable.

He leaned against the sink as the memories swelled inside him. The gentle ache in his chest erupted into heated stabs that threatened to slice his heart into pieces.

The images swirling in his head darkened as the nightmare he'd lived over and over for almost two decades took front and center: Helene's body in a pool of blood, faceup, her head against the hearth, her beautiful locks of hair matted with crimson.

The pain became blinding and this time much too physical. Troy clutched his chest as he stumbled backward, falling against the scarred wooden table. Each beat of his heart was agony.

Then reality checked in. This was more than grief. He was having a coronary attack.

There was a knock at the door as he tried to drag himself to the phone. The door was unlocked, as it usually was on the ranch. He waited, hoping it was Dylan. But there was no reason to think his son would return tonight.

He heard a child's voice, or maybe he was hallucinating.

He fell over a chair and the crash reverberated through the house.

"Troy, are you in there? Are you okay?"

The voice was female, vaguely familiar. He tried to answer, but all he managed was a guttural moan.

"Troy, what's wrong?"

He looked up and into the eyes of Eve Worthington. Now he was certain he was hallucinating. The last person who'd be coming to his rescue was the young psychiatrist who'd worked so hard to pull him from his emotional shell while he was in prison.

"Please tell me what's wrong. Is it your heart?"

His response was choked by the pain.

"Hang in here with me, Troy. I'm calling an ambulance."

The room began to spin. He tried to focus on Eve, only to have her disappear in a swirl of darkness.

He wouldn't die. He couldn't. Not until he found Helene's killer. He would not fail her again.

"WHAT'S WRONG WITH HIM, Momma? Is he dying?"

"Shh, Joey. He's sick. We have to help him."

Troy muttered something unintelligible.

She leaned in closer so that she could hear him better.

"Dylan," he gasped. "Call Dylan."

Dylan—the son Gordon Epps had mentioned. "I'll get him," she said, her fingers already punching in 911 on her unfamiliar cell phone. Once she was assured medical help was on the way, she glanced around the room and spotted Troy's cell phone on the kitchen table.

She left Troy's side long enough to get it. It took only a second to find Dylan's number amidst Troy's limited contacts. He answered on the second ring.

"What's up, Dad?"

"This isn't Troy, but I'm with him. I think he's having a heart attack. I've called an ambulance, but he's asking for you." The words tumbled out of her mouth. She wasn't even sure she was making sense.

"Who is this?"

"I'm just a friend who happened to drop in. Troy's in a lot of pain and barely conscious."

"I'll be right there."

"I'm scared, Momma. Let's go home."

She looked at her son. "We can't go yet, sweetie." She held out a hand and he inched toward her, clearly frightened of Troy.

"Eve." Troy's speech was clearer, but sweat beaded on his brow and his breathing was still labored.

"I'm right here, Troy."

"Orson…"

"Yeah." She cradled Troy's head in her arms. "He's escaped."

"Dangerous… Stay safe."

"I will." Even in the panic of a heart attack, Troy was worried about her. That was so like him. Thank God, she'd shown up when she did.

Joey tugged on her arm. She tried to pull him down beside her, but he backed away. "Is that a bad man?"

"No. He's my friend."

The words didn't convince Joey, and she couldn't do much to make him feel safe until the emergency was over. Fortunately, the door flew open minutes later and a good-looking man in jeans rushed in, still pulling on his shirt. An attractive woman with flaming red hair followed right behind.

She stood and moved away so that they could squeeze in beside Troy. "I'm Eve Worthington, an old friend of your father's. I just—" The scream of an approaching ambulance drowned out the rest of her words.

Dylan took over from there and the next few minutes passed in a blur of activity. Joey began to tremble as the house filled with strangers and medics who worked quickly to get Troy onto the gurney and into the ambulance. Eve held on to his shaking hand, tugging him out of the way and giving assurances as best she could amid the chaos.

Both Dylan and Collette Ledger were so engrossed in their concern for Troy that they simply accepted her explanation as being an old friend without question. It wasn't until Dylan had thanked her profusely and rushed to follow the ambulance to the hospital that she had a minute to reflect on her own situation.

It wasn't good. Once she'd realized that the police weren't taking concerns for her and Joey's safety seriously, she decided to take Gordon's advice and pay Troy a visit. She really hadn't thought beyond that.

For the first time since she'd arrived on the scene, Eve really looked at Collette Ledger. Even in sweatpants, she was striking, with thick red hair that fell in loose curls about her shoulders and a faultless complexion.

Eve suspected they were near the same age,

though Collette could easily be a few years younger than her thirty-one years.

"I'm so thankful you dropped by," Collette said. "I hate to think what might have happened if you hadn't shown up when you did."

"I'm glad I was here, too," Eve said. "Believe me, my timing is not usually that good."

"You're not from this area, are you?"

"No. I live in Dallas."

"I didn't think I'd seen you around town before. How do you know Troy?"

"From prison."

"Really? Prison."

"I was his psychiatrist."

"You don't look like a psyche. Not that you looked like an inmate. I mean…"

"It's okay," Eve assured her. "We're both a little shaken now."

"That's for sure. I don't know what your experience with Troy has been, but I'm guessing it was good, or you wouldn't be here."

"I'm very fond of him," Eve said.

"So am I, Collette agreed. "He's difficult to get to know, but once he opens up to you, you can't help but like him. And no matter what anyone says, I know he didn't kill his wife. Dylan realizes that, too."

"I agree," Eve said.

"I'm glad we're on the same page here. Troy didn't mention that you were stopping by tonight."

"I was going to surprise him," Eve said. Shock him was more like it. And ask him if she could stay with him a few days. That was out of the question now. There was no reason to get into any of that with Collette, though.

"I'll be going now," Eve said. "There's nothing more I can do here except get in the way."

"Where are you going?"

An excellent question that Eve couldn't honestly answer. She'd had no backup plan. Eve quickly considered her options. "Joey and I are on our way to visit friends in Austin," she lied.

Joey tugged on the hem of her shirt. "You said we were going to a ranch."

"We did. This is it. Now we're off to the rest of our adventure."

"There's no need to rush off," Collette said. "If you're half as shaken as I am, you're in no shape to drive. And I could really use the company. I hate the thought of waiting alone for news about Troy. I'll make coffee."

"Coffee sounds good. And I do think I'm still in a bit of shock."

Collette filled the pot with water from the tap and spooned the grinds into the filter. "I'm so worried about my father-in-law that I can barely measure the water."

"Troy's tough. If anyone can pull through a heart attack, it's him," Eve said, unconsciously falling into the psychiatrist role. Not that they were certain Troy had a heart attack, but it had certainly appeared to be a coronary trauma.

"Have you had dinner?" Collette asked. "I'm not sure what Troy has in his fridge, but I have leftover roast beef and gravy at my house, or I could make you a salad. And I'm sure we could rustle up the makings of a peanut butter and jelly sandwich at either house, if Joey would prefer that."

"Thanks, but we've had dinner." Joey had eaten half a sandwich and a few apple slices in the car. That qualified as a major meal for him. As for herself, she hadn't eaten anything all day except a half slice of toast and a few cashews she'd munched in the car. Her stomach had been in no condition for food after the morning's call from Gordon. Her insides were even shakier now.

"What's your son's name?" Collette asked.

"You probably said already, but it didn't register in the bedlam."

Eve rested her hands on his shoulders. "This is Joey."

"Hi, Joey."

The boy mumbled a hello, his eyes downcast.

"Joey. I like that name," Collette said. "Would you like to watch TV? I can probably find the cartoon channel if you'll help me."

Joey nodded, but scrunched himself against Eve's leg as if Collette had threatened a time-out.

"He's shy around strangers," Eve said, wishing that was all that kept him glued to her.

"Can't blame him for being a little cautious, considering what we've been dealing with tonight. Why don't you get him settled in the family room? I'll bring the coffee when it's brewed."

"Thanks."

Joey clung to her leg, his thin fingers digging into the fabric of her trousers as he shadowed her to the couch. By the time she found a channel he liked, Collette was returning with the coffee, a glass of milk and two oatmeal cookies that appeared to be homemade. Collette set the milk and cookies near Joey.

He mumbled a thank-you, and smiled timidly, staring at Collette from beneath his dark lashes. Eve experienced another wave of uneasiness that bordered on panic. They would have been safe here, even if Orson did still have the crazy notion of coming after her. It was certainly the kind of thing that a manipulative, revengeful person like Orson would do. Now her only option would be a stuffy hotel, and even taking Joey to a park would involve risk.

She and Collette moved to chairs near the window, still in Joey's sight, but not so close that he'd hear every word, even if he had been listening. Fortunately, he appeared lost in a cartoon.

Eve supplied the most basic facts about her relationship with Troy—that he had become a friend as well as a patient when she had served as his therapist during his incarceration. She'd stopped working at the prison two years ago and hadn't seen Troy since that time. She felt remiss for not getting in touch with him sooner.

"I wish everyone saw Troy as you do," Collette said. "Too many people around here still see him as a murderer. Troy never complains, but I know the suspicions and mistrust take their toll. I think it hurts him most that his sons have avoided seeing him since his release—except for Dylan, of course."

"Troy always talked a lot about his sons."

"He will be so sorry he missed visiting with you."

The conversation turned to less stressful topics. Ranch life. The house Dylan and Collette had just built. Helene's treasured courtyard garden that Collette had restored with Dylan and Troy's help. Life in the small town of Mustang Run.

When Colette's phone rang, Eve was surprised to see that an hour had passed since the ambulance had sped away with Troy inside.

Collette pulled the phone from her pocket and checked the caller ID. "It's Dylan."

The tension seemed to melt from Collette's features as she talked, allowing Eve to breathe easier. She stood and took their coffee cups to the sink, giving Collette a little privacy. For once, Joey didn't follow.

Collette was smiling when she joined her in the kitchen. "They're still running tests, but Troy is responding to treatment and meds. He's conscious and talking."

"Thank goodness."

Moisture brimmed in Collette's eyes. "It would have been so sad if Troy had lost his life just when he was finding it again. I just hope his other sons give him a chance the way Dylan has."

"Maybe tonight's incident will open their eyes," Eve said.

"I wouldn't bet on it, but I'm sure Dylan will let them know about it. Anyway, Dylan said Troy remembers that you were here, and he's asked about you."

She'd almost hoped he wouldn't remember. He didn't need to waste his energy worrying about her.

"He seems to be under the impression that you're in some kind of trouble," Collette said.

"I'm sure I didn't say anything to give him that impression."

"Still, Dylan says he seems anxious to see you. I know this is an imposition, but is there any way you could make a quick trip to the hospital in the morning? It would mean a lot to him."

"I'm not sure." She wasn't even sure she'd stay in Austin. Perhaps the best thing now would be to just go home and rely on the police for protection.

"You could stay the night," Collette said. "Then you wouldn't have to drive these unfamiliar country roads in the dark."

"You mean stay here at the ranch?"

"Sure, there's lots of room," Colette said. "It's not fancy, but it's comfortable. I'd invite you to stay with Dylan and me, but unfortunately we haven't furnished the guest room as yet."

Staying here was the perfect solution. Even if Orson was still planning revenge, he wouldn't show up here. And by morning Orson might be behind bars again.

"I suppose I could stay tonight," she said, trying not to sound too enthusiastic. "If you're sure Troy won't mind."

"After you saved his life? Not that he'd mind anyway. I'll help you get your things out of the car and show you to the guest rooms. All the beds have new mattresses and linens, so you can take your pick."

"I can manage the luggage. I'll just bring in an overnight bag."

"Then I'll straighten the kitchen. Oh, but first give me your cell phone number in case I need to get in touch with you about Troy.

That way you won't have to bother picking up the house phone if it rings and answering a hundred questions if someone calls for Troy. And I'll give you my number in case you need something in the house that you can't locate."

Eve was hesitant to give Collette her phone number. The phone was new, temporary, bought with cash at a convenience store to make certain Orson could not use it to track her down. It had been purchased right after she'd gone to the bank and withdrawn five thousand dollars so that she wouldn't have to use her credit cards.

The only one who had the phone number was Gordon Epps—and the ambulance service, if they bothered to check their incoming call records.

But surely Collette could be trusted.

Once they'd exchanged numbers, Eve took her car keys from her pocket and started to her car. Joey jumped off the couch when he saw her pass with her keys in hand.

"I'll be right back, sweetie. You can keep watching TV. I'm just going to the car to get our luggage."

"What about our adventure?"

"It's late, and I'm very tired. We'll spend the night and get an early start in the morning."

"I don't want to spend the night here. I wanna sleep in my bed."

"Your bed is all the way back in Dallas. Besides, this is your first visit to a real ranch."

"And in the morning, I'll show you the cows and the horses," Colette said. "Do you like horses?"

"I think so. I never got close to one," he said, hurrying to keep up with Eve as she started toward the car. "But I need to go home."

Eve stooped and hugged him. "It's going to be okay, Joey. You'll like it here, and I'll sleep next to you."

"Promise?"

"I promise."

The howl of coyotes in the distance and the forlorn hoot of an owl greeted them as they stepped onto the porch. Dark shadows jumped out at her as she took the creaking steps to the walk. Weirdly, she had a chilling feeling that someone was watching her.

It was just the isolation of the ranch and the fear that stalked her. She couldn't give in to it. Yet the icy trepidation stayed with her until she and Joey were back inside the well-lit house.

She'd be safe here. To believe otherwise in the face of the facts would be letting Orson Bastion win the battle of minds without him ever making a move against her.

She was tougher than that.

THE CREAKS AND RASPS of the rambling old ranch house set Eve's nerves on edge. Surprisingly, the same had not been true for Joey. He'd fallen asleep mere minutes after she'd tucked him into a twin bed at the end of the long hallway.

Once she was sure he was sleeping soundly, Eve left him to brush her teeth and wash and cream her face in the nearby bathroom.

Thoughts of Orson continued to plague Eve's mind as she slipped into her cotton pajamas. Of all the inmates she'd counseled, he'd been the only one she dreaded having to talk to—even before the night he'd left no doubt that he could kill her without a second's remorse.

Joey was still sleeping soundly when she returned to the bedroom, but anxiety was buzzing inside Eve like a horde of angry bumblebees. Knowing sleep wouldn't come quickly, she went back to the family room and turned on the TV.

The local news was coming up next. Great. If they'd just announce that Orson Bastion had been recaptured, her nightmare could end and she could not only get a good night's sleep, but actually look forward to seeing Troy in the morning.

She shed her slippers and stretched out on the brown leather sofa while a string of commercials aired. Finally the screen switched to the newsroom of a local channel.

"Stay tuned for breaking news concerning escaped convict Orson Bastion."

Eve tensed and waited. When a sophisticated blond anchor appeared, the grim expression on her meticulously made-up face guaranteed the news would be disturbing.

"A young woman was fatally strangled after being kidnapped from a Dallas shopping center this afternoon. Her car was found deserted a few hours later. Police suspect that escaped prisoner Orson Bastion may have been involved in the death."

Eve clutched a throw pillow to her chest and fought off a bout of nausea. Orson had killed again, which was exactly what she'd testified he'd do if he was released from prison.

He'd exhibited so many behaviors consistent with that of a psychopath, especially the lack of emotional involvement with others. The only thing that was missing was the fact that he didn't have a real history of criminal behavior; or, if he did, she hadn't been made aware of it.

He was in jail for killing his stepbrother in an act of rage. He'd only received a charge of second-degree murder. Orson had been twenty-eight years old at the time. He was forty now.

Eve flicked off the TV. She didn't need to hear more. Gordon had said Orson would never look for her at the Ledger ranch, but what if Gordon was wrong? Still, this was likely the safest place on the planet, at least for the time being.

If Troy were here, she'd likely feel totally safe, but she was alone in this rambling old house, without so much as a weapon to protect her son.

She walked to the kitchen, checked the drawers and took out a carving knife. Just in case. Not that she'd need it. Still, knife in hand, she wandered back into the den just as streams of light flicked across the window. The low hum of an engine purred and then stopped.

Someone was here, parked in the driveway.

Surely not Orson. He couldn't have found her this quickly. Yet adrenaline pumped through her leaving her shaking so violently she had to hold the knife with both hands.

Heavy footsteps clumped across the wooden porch. Eve fought the rising panic. She had to stay calm. She could do this. She had to do this. If the man outside the door was Orson, a lock would never deter him.

She stood so that she'd be behind the door if it opened, poised to bury the blade of the knife in Orson's back the minute he stepped inside—if it was Orson.

She heard the flick of a key in the lock. If the person at the door had a key, surely it wasn't Orson. The knob turned, the door opened and the intruder stepped across the threshold.

His breathing was deep and sharp. His voice echoed though the room.

"The day of reckoning has finally come."

Chapter Four

The voice proclaiming the fatalistic message was masculine, husky. Unfamiliar.

The intruder reached for the door and slammed it shut, leaving her and the knife in full view.

Her knees buckled and her breath rushed out in a whoosh. This wasn't Orson. Instead, it was hunk of a cowboy who reeked of strength and power.

Before she could say anything, he grabbed the arm holding the knife, yanked it over her head and shoved her against the wall. She struggled to push him away, but she might as well have been flailing against a brick wall. A brick wall with broad shoulders that smelled of musk and forest glens.

"Take your hands off me," she sputtered.

"After you tell me what the hell is going on here."

"I thought you were someone else." Her relief drowned in a rush of confusing awareness, as the man's breath heated a spot just below her right earlobe. His masculinity was staggering. She gasped and gulped for air.

"Who are you?" he demanded.

"I'm a friend of Troy's. Now back off before I—"

"Before you what, come at me with a knife?"

She writhed and tried again to break free, but he strengthened his hold on her wrists and kept his body pressed against hers.

Finally, she shifted so that she was staring straight into the depths of his dark eyes at extremely close range. Something jumped inside her, an eruption of emotions that under the circumstances made no sense at all.

His hold loosened, as if whatever had left her quaking had affected him as well. "I'll take that knife," he said. "And then you can tell me who you are and why you're defending my father's house like it was the Holy Grail."

Anxiety swelled again. This didn't add up. "You're lying," she said. "I met Troy's son earlier tonight."

"You may have met Dylan. I'm Sean, the

mild-mannered offspring with a cool head. Lucky for you."

She saw the resemblance now. He looked even more like Troy than Dylan did. The same slightly squared jawline. The same classic nose. Only, Sean was years younger than Troy, and so ruggedly handsome that he could have been a soap opera star. And he was still so close that he could probably feel her heart beating.

Collette had said that Troy's other sons were estranged from their father. But then Dylan must have called them when he left for the hospital. Maybe his having a heart attack had gotten through to at least one of Troy's other sons.

"If you talked to Dylan, he must have told you I was here," she said, still trying to make sense of this.

"He mentioned a friend had found Dad. He didn't say you were staying here. In fact, he made a point of telling me the house would be empty and the spare key was under the flowerpot next to the door. So what are you doing here?"

"If you'll release me, I'll explain." She wouldn't, of course, but she'd tell him all he needed to know.

"Deal. As soon as you let go of the knife."

She exhaled sharply and released her killer grasp on it. Before he moved away, his right hand slid slowly down her left arm. Awareness vibrated through her.

"Mommy! Mommy!" She made a quick return to the harsh reality of the situation, as Joey's high-pitched calls echoed down the hallway.

"My son," she said. "He has nightmares."

Sean cocked his head to the side and arched his brows. "Your son. A husband? A daughter? Exactly how many people are in this house?"

"Just my son, Joey, and me. I don't have a husband and Joey's an only child."

She was babbling in her relief. Whatever complications Sean presented would be minuscule compared to what she'd have faced had it been Orson instead of Troy's son who'd showed up tonight.

"Momma!" The cry had become more hysterical.

"I'm coming, sweetie."

She hurried away without further explanation, grateful to break away from Sean Ledger and get her emotions back under control.

In the two years since Brock's death she

hadn't once felt the pangs of attraction for another man. She'd begun to worry that she never would. Now was not the time for fate to turn up the heat.

SEAN WATCHED EVE WORTHINGTON hurry down the hall and disappear into what had once been his bedroom. She was the last thing he'd expected to find when he pushed through the heavy door of his childhood home.

Before encountering her, his head had been swimming in a thick fog of memories. The good, the bad and the tragic had immersed him so deeply into the past that his feet had felt like lead when he climbed the steps to the porch.

Nothing like a woman about to plunge a knife into your back to smack you back into the present. *But what in the hell was a woman and kid doing here?*

Dylan had written several times about their father and the fact that he was settling into the life of a rancher. Not once had he mentioned that Troy had a lady friend—one young enough to be his daughter. If he had, Sean would have never come home again.

He'd been only thirteen years old when his mother was murdered in this very house. His world had been destroyed that day. Then, when his father had been accused of the crime, Sean literally wanted to die.

When his brothers were asleep that night, he'd taken one of his dad's guns and actually placed the barrel of it into his mouth. He might have pulled the trigger if his imagination hadn't played ghostly tricks on his mind, probably an easy feat, considering his shaky emotional state.

He saw his mother that night as clearly as he saw the weapon in his hands. She'd stepped into the room and taken the gun from his shaky hands. It had fallen to the floor without a sound. He'd tried to hold on to his mother, but she dissolved like a warm breath on a frosty morning.

He never told anyone about that, had tried to block it from his own mind. But there had been many nights when those memories were so vivid that he could feel the chill of the evaporating vapor and taste the cold metallic bitterness of the gun barrel.

He shouldn't have come back here. Returning to Willow Creek Ranch had worked for Dylan, but there was no way Sean would ever mend fences with his father or become totally convinced of his innocence.

He'd visit his father in the hospital in the morning, but then he'd be on his way. In fact, he should probably apologize to Eve Worthington for barging in on her and leave right now, before he looked into those gorgeous, haunted eyes of hers again.

He started down the hall after Eve, hating the memories that the house awakened. He stopped near the doorway where she'd disappeared. Her voice was soft and reassuring when she talked to her child, yet there was a shudder of fear in its depths, likely the same fear that had initiated her waiting at the door with a knife.

She'd thought he was someone else, obviously someone she was deathly afraid of. A stalker? An ex-husband? A betrayed lover?

None of his business and not his problem. He was running from woman trouble, not looking for it.

He stopped, just out of sight of Eve and her complaining son.

"I wanna go home."

"It's too far to drive back to Dallas tonight. Besides, you don't want to miss the fun of seeing the horses, do you?"

"What if I don't like horses?"

If she was from Dallas, then why hadn't

Dylan realized she was spending the night? Perhaps he'd just forgotten with all that was going on with Troy. Still, it was odd he hadn't remembered it when he told him to make himself at home. Sean turned and walked back to the kitchen.

He opened the refrigerator and pulled out a beer. He'd barely swallowed his first swig when his cell phone rang. It was Dylan. Sean didn't bother with a hello. "What the hell have you gotten me into in now?"

"I take it that means you've arrived at the ranch and met Eve Worthington."

"I met her all right. She threw me a welcoming party, only instead of balloons, she was wielding a knife."

There was a short pause in the phone conversation in which Sean overheard a muttered thanks from Dylan.

"Sorry, bro," Dylan said. "One of the nurses just brought me a cup of coffee. What's this about a knife?"

"Dad's houseguest took me for an intruder and came at me with a kitchen knife. I had to take it away from her."

"Still fighting off the women."

"You're smiling, aren't you?"

"Maybe just a little. Why'd she have a knife?"

"She thought I was someone else."

"Probably believes all that bunk about the house being haunted."

"Our house is haunted?"

"So some of the locals say. Anyway, I'm sure Eve's fear was no match for your Ledger brawn and charm. Apologize to her for the confusion."

"As soon as you explain why you failed to warn me the house was occupied."

"I just found out myself. I called Collette to tell her you were in town, and she said she'd persuaded Eve to spend the night. That's why I'm calling, hoping to give you fair warning. Collette is calling Eve, probably has her on the phone now."

"A little after the fact."

"You know, you have to take some of the blame," Dylan said. "You could have called and said you were coming *before* you reached Mustang Run. Then we could have avoided the surprise element."

"I wasn't sure I'd actually go through with the visit, until I saw the city limits sign."

Even after he'd made the call to Dylan, he still might have turned around and driven the other way if Dylan hadn't told him about Troy's coronary attack.

"Why are you still at the hospital?" Sean asked. "You said you were leaving for the night the last time we talked. Troy's not having any new problems, is he?"

"No. Dad's resting now. The cardiologist on staff stopped by the room. He says the prognosis is good for a complete recovery, though nothing is guaranteed. I'm heading that way now. Do you need anything?"

"A few answers. What's the deal between Dad and Eve?"

"Hard to say. The situation being what it is, I haven't had a chance to get the full story from either of them. Apparently, they became friends when she was his prison psychiatrist a few years back. She said she was just passing through tonight and decided to stop in and see him. Just in time to save his life, I might add."

"Then they're not a romantic item?"

"Man, Sean. Where did you get an idea like that? She's our age. She has a kid, probably a husband as well."

"There is no husband. And what did you expect me to think? I show up, and she's here in her pajamas."

"In her pajamas, huh? That must have spiced up the knife removal routine."

"I was defending, not groping."

"Whatever. But don't read any more into this than is actually there. Eve said she was passing through. No reason not to believe her."

"Then she didn't mention that she was in any kind of trouble?"

"No, but now that you mention it, Dad seemed anxious about not getting to talk to her."

"Did he say why?"

"No. He's been pretty much incoherent all night, first from the coronary trauma and then from the meds."

"Okay. We'll talk more when I see you."

"I'm dead tired. Do you mind if we put off our reunion until morning? Collette and I will come down and cook you, Eve and the boy an old-time ranch breakfast."

"Sounds like a winner. I guess I can round up some linens and a pillow around this place?"

"Take your old room. The beds are made."

"And occupied."

"Then avoid temptation and find another room."

"There is no temptation involved."

"Then just make yourself at home. And, Sean, I'm really glad you're here. It will mean a lot to Dad."

Sean doubted that. He said a quick good-bye.

Once he'd finished the beer, he checked the rest of the fridge's contents. Choices weren't bad.

He found bread in the pantry and made himself a ham and cheese sandwich, then poured a tall glass of milk to wash it down. Halfway through the meal, he heard the soft patter of footsteps in the hallway.

He looked up as Eve joined him in the kitchen. She'd pulled a pale blue robe over her pajamas. That did nothing to hide the fact that she was a damned attractive woman.

She looked around the kitchen, her gaze focusing on the sandwich fixings he'd left on the counter.

"Help yourself," he said. "Bread's fresh and the ham is good. There's plenty of beer, or milk if you're a purist."

"I'm not opposed to cold beer, but a glass of milk sounds better tonight."

"Something to soothe the savage beast."

A blush flushed her cheeks. "I'm not

ordinarily so savage. I'm a city girl. I guess I let the isolation get to me."

"Looked like a little more than that to me."

"Look, Sean, I'm really sorry about the knife incident, but can we just forget about it now?"

"Subject closed." For the time being. "There's hot chocolate mix in the pantry."

She nodded. "That sounds even better. Can I make a cup for you?"

"Sure. Why not?"

She turned back to face him, and her straight, shiny brown locks seductively bounced around the bottom of her chin. Much *too* seductively.

He finished off his sandwich and wiped his mouth on the paper towel he'd been using as a napkin, just as she started to the table with two steaming mugs of cocoa in hand.

"Sorry, but I didn't find marshmallows," she said.

"I suspect Troy is not a marshmallow kind of guy," Sean said. "But then, you evidently know him much better than I do."

She stared into her cup for a moment and then lifted her eyes to meet his. Hers were the color of warm cognac, vibrant even in the fluorescent light from the overhead fixture.

"I was Troy's prison psychiatrist for a couple of years."

"Dylan told me. He called while you were calming your son."

"Collette called me as well. She explained everything. I'm truly sorry for intruding on your homecoming."

"Actually, I'm more the intruder. You were the invited guest."

"It's your home."

"*Was* my home. When I was thirteen. I've hung my hat in a lot of places since then."

"Nonetheless, Joey and I will clear out of your way in the morning."

"Don't leave on my account. It's a big house, and I don't plan to be here long."

Her shoulders squared. "You should. You owe it to your father to get to know the man he is today."

He bristled a bit at the preachy tone, especially when she had no idea what she was talking about. "Do you always offer your opinion to people you've just met?"

"No," she admitted. "I seldom give advice at all anymore."

Her shoulders and voice fell as if he'd sucker

punched her. It gave him no pleasure. "It's okay," he said. "My dad and I have issues."

She merely nodded, leaving lots of questions in his mind about just what his father had told her about him and his brothers. Had Troy played her, fed her what he thought she'd like to hear in order to make an impression on her? Or had she just dug around in his mind and come up with her own conclusions?

She finished her hot chocolate, stood and carried her empty cup to the sink. Once she rinsed it, she turned back to him. "Again, I'm sorry for the knife incident, and I wish you and Troy the best."

He watched her walk away, her slim hips swaying just enough to make her exit interesting. He thought again of the way her body had felt pressed against his. For a minute back there, he'd had the crazy urge to kiss her.

The urge surfaced again, and he wondered what she'd do if he followed her to the bedroom door and kissed her good-night.

Probably come at him with a knife while he slept.

He'd leave well enough alone before he became as lust-craved as Laci Cahill. With one big difference. He wasn't married—and had no intention of ever playing the matrimony game.

EVE PULLED THE COVERS about Joey and leaned close, letting her lips brush his forehead. Asleep, innocence was etched into his youthful face. If only she could give him that simple purity of joy back again, instead of dragging him back into the ominous threat of peril.

Trepidation played havoc with her breathing as she backed away from Joey's bed. What if that had been Orson at the door tonight? What if he'd been the man who'd pinned her to the wall with his brute strength? The truth shuddered through her.

There would have been no way she could have protected Joey.

But it hadn't been Orson Bastion. It had been Sean Ledger, whose hard, unrelenting strength held her captive. Yet, the minute she'd realized he wasn't dangerous, it had been attraction, not fear, she'd felt at his hands.

Eve slipped out of her robe, draped it across the one chair in the room and then dropped to the twin bed opposite Joey's. She slid beneath the crisp sheets and pulled the quilt over her as confusing thoughts tumbled through her mind.

The dread that had chilled her before Sean's arrival had disappeared. The rambling old house no longer made her uneasy. If anything, she felt protected. Sean made the difference.

Yet, she couldn't start relying on him. Tomorrow might bring anything. Tonight she needed to get some sleep.

Her eyelids grew heavy, and she turned over to stare out the window and into the darkness, and the scatter of stars that studded the sky.

Her mind flashed back to Sean and a rush of heat crept inside her.

Surely not desire, she told herself. Not in this situation. If she felt anything at all for Sean, the attraction stemmed from pure relief that he wasn't Orson Bastion.

If he had been, she'd be dead.

But Orson was still on the loose.

SOMEONE WAS IN THE HOUSE. Eve could hear him breathing, smell the odors of sweat and cheap aftershave, see his shadow coming nearer.

She clutched the knife and felt the sear of pain and hot, sticky blood gushing into her hand. When she looked down she saw that the handle was missing and the blade had sliced into her palm.

Her brain began to clatter. Eve jerked awake and sat up in bed. The clattering wasn't in her brain, but was coming from the bedside table where her cell phone was vibrating against the old wood.

She glanced at the clock as she grabbed the phone to quiet it before it woke Joey. Five minutes before six in the morning was extremely early for a call from either Gordon or Collette, and they were the only two who had her number.

The vibration in the palm of her hand mirrored the state of her nerves as she whispered hello.

"It's Gordon. Is this Eve?"

"Yes." The urgency in his voice told her this was not a good-news call.

Chapter Five

Eve tried to steady the phone in her shaky hand as she untangled herself from the bed covers.

"I can barely hear you," Gordon said. "Are you okay?"

"I'm fine."

"Where are you?"

"Hold on."

She slid her legs over the side of the bed and padded into the hall, quietly closing the bedroom door behind her before resuming the conversation. "I'm sorry, Gordon. I should have called you and let you know I was all right. I took your suggestion. I'm at Troy Ledger's ranch in Mustang Run."

"Thank God for that. Troy is the one man who'll understand your situation. How is he?"

"He's in the hospital." She told him how

she'd arrived to find him in the throes of an apparent heart attack.

"Good thing you showed up when you did," Gordon said.

"I'm taking that as a good omen, but I'm still worried about Troy."

"Are you alone in Troy's house?"

"Not exactly. Troy's son Sean is here."

"You mean Dylan?"

"No, it seems I wasn't the only one who showed up at the ranch unexpectedly last evening. It's complicated."

"Sounds that way. The good news is you're safe and don't have to worry about Orson showing up at your house."

And yet she could hear the alarm in Gordon's voice. "Is there news about Orson?"

The long pause sent her pulse spiraling.

"This could mean nothing, Eve. There's no conclusive proof that Orson is even still in Texas."

"Don't beat around the bush. Just give me the truth."

"Okay. I don't know if you've heard, but a young woman was killed yesterday in a carjacking, and the police seem to think Orson might have been involved."

"I caught just the basics on the evening news last night."

"Then you know the car was deserted a few miles from where you live."

"No, I didn't realize that." A new wave of uneasiness wrecked havoc with her control. For all she knew, Orson might have already been to her house looking for her. Had she been there…

She forced herself to breathe. "Is there more?"

"Reagan Conner has been trying to get in touch with you."

"Reagan Conner? Should I know who that is?"

"He's the homicide detective investigating the murder."

"Why would he contact you?"

"To see if I know anything to help them locate Orson. He questioned me about former inmates that Orson might try to hook up with for help in getting out of the area. I gave him a few names, but also told him about the threats on your life."

"Did Detective Conner mention that I'd called the police department yesterday and told them I could be a target?"

"Yes. He wanted my take on the threat

Orson made to you, but for the record, he thinks you're overreacting. He's convinced Orson's only concern will be avoiding capture. Nonetheless, he says he's been trying to reach you."

"Did you give him this number?"

"No. You asked me not to give it to anyone, and I wouldn't go against your wishes without asking first. I think you should call him, but handle it anyway you want. Just don't go home until Orson is back in prison, or the cops are certain he's out of the area."

"Thanks for the heads-up that he was near my neighborhood. You can be sure I won't go home until I'm convinced it's safe to do so."

Not that she had any idea where she would go, now that she couldn't stay here.

"Just hang tight," Gordon said. "Every cop in the state is on the lookout for him. He'll be behind bars soon."

"I'm counting on that."

In the meantime, Orson was disrupting every aspect of her life. If she didn't have Joey, she'd just buy a gun and take her chances with the monster back in Dallas.

But she did have Joey. Violence had torn his life apart once. Now she not only had to protect him, but see that he was not traumatized again.

Once they'd said their goodbyes, anxiety scratched along her raw nerves like the claws of a wildcat. She drooped against the wall and buried her head in her hands, massaging her temples, as if that would stimulate her brain into making a decision as to what she should do next.

"Is there a problem?"

Sean's voice startled her. She turned to find him a few feet away, shadowed in the moonlight that filtered into the house. He was wearing jeans, still unsnapped at the waist. No shirt. No shoes.

She fought an impulse to throw herself into his strong arms and stay there until the quaking inside stopped. After the knife episode, surely he'd think she was nuts. She managed to keep a ragged hold on her composure.

"How much did you hear?" she asked.

"Enough to know it wasn't good news."

"Good news seldom comes at daybreak, does it?"

"Not often. Anything I can do to help?"

"No, but thanks for asking."

"I'm a good listener. Actually, I'm not," he

admitted, "but I'll make a stab at it, since we're both awake anyway."

"Believe me, you don't want to get involved in this."

"In that case, can I offer a shoulder to cry on?"

"That's the most tempting offer I've had in days." Maybe years, but she wouldn't go there. "But crying wouldn't help."

He propped a hand next to her shoulder, leaning against the wall, not pinning her in as he'd done before, yet so close she could feel the titillating warmth of his body.

Maybe it was just the act of standing this close to a half-dressed hunk when the sun hadn't even peeked over the horizon, but she seemed to be forgetting how to breathe.

"Who did you think I was when you came at me with the knife?" Sean asked.

"I don't know. A burglar, I guess. Didn't we go over this before?"

"Are you sure you're not running from someone?"

"That's a ludicrous idea."

He cupped her chin in his right hand, tilting her head so that she had to meet his piercing gaze head-on. "I know fear when I see it, Eve. Even in people."

"I'm not afraid," she lied. "I'm concerned about a friend. That's all. I'm really tired and I'd like a few more hours sleep before I have to get up."

"Have it your way. If you change your mind, I'm in the room right across the hall. And remember, you don't have to rush off in the morning just because Troy isn't here. I'm not going to seduce you or try to take advantage of you, you know."

Intentional or not, she was already being seduced. Apparently all it took in her current state of mind was a gentle touch and a wallop of masculinity.

But even if she was attracted to Sean, she couldn't stay. Troy had enough problems, without having to worry himself with her. In fact, even visiting Troy in the hospital would be a mistake. She wouldn't get into that with Sean, either. She'd just get up in a few hours and clear out.

It was the only sensible and considerate thing to do.

Yet, it was all she could do not to run after Sean and take him up on the offer of one of his broad, muscular shoulders to cry on, as she watched him walk away.

SEAN SOAKED UP HIS remaining cream gravy with the last bite of his second biscuit. "Eggs, steak, hash browns, gravy and biscuits. Now, that's what I call a breakfast."

"Takes a hearty breakfast to keep a cowboy going," Dylan said.

"You've definitely synced into this ranching lifestyle," Sean said.

"Does that surprise you?"

Sean nodded. "Yeah. Lost my bet with Wyatt. I said you'd never last a week back in Mustang Run."

"So you and our older brother were betting on my falling out of the saddle. Too bad I didn't get in on any of that money."

"I'd have changed my bet if I'd known you'd luck into meeting a gorgeous woman who makes heavenly biscuits." Sean tipped his coffee mug toward Collette.

She smiled and tossed her head, so that her wild halo of red hair resettled around her shoulders. "Thank you. You are now officially my favorite brother-in-law."

"Only because you've never met the others," Sean assured her.

Sean wiped his mouth on the plaid napkin and leaned back in his chair. The others were through eating, though all five of them continued to linger at the marred kitchen table. Everyone's plates except Eve's and Joey's were empty. Joey had eaten half a biscuit and a few bites of scrambled egg. Eve's food was practically untouched.

She seemed distracted, troubled. He was still certain she was running scared, but she clearly didn't want his help. Fine, she wasn't his problem. He should just let it go at that.

"I'm heading into the hospital as soon as we finish here," Dylan said. "Why don't you ride in with me, Sean? I want to be there to see the look on Dad's face when he sees you for the first time in seventeen years."

Sean dreaded the moment. The last time he'd seen his father, the judge had just issued the sentence of life in prison. Sean had been sitting in the courtroom with his brothers and his grandparents. His grandfather had lifted a fist a victory. His grandmother had cried and proclaimed justice had been served, but it wouldn't bring back her beautiful Helene.

The heartbreaking disappointment of that day was firmly implanted in Sean's mind. Until then, he'd prayed for a miracle that would prove his dad hadn't killed his mother.

His prayers had died along with a large part of his heart that day. All he'd gotten in answer was an almost blank stare from his father before the security officer led him away.

Not once in all the years since had his father reached out to him; so why the hell would Troy Ledger give a damn about seeing him now?

He drained the last of his coffee. "I'm not sure that the shock of seeing me would be the best medicine for Troy in his condition. Maybe I should just postpone the reunion for a few days."

"I think having you there is exactly what Dad needs," Dylan protested. "Besides, I don't trust you to stick around long before the neigh of a distant horse lures you away."

"I haven't even checked out the neighs on this ranch yet. I could stay around here and do that this morning."

"Where is the hospital?" Eve asked.

"It's Carlton-Hayes Regional Hospital, near Austin."

"Not my favorite place," Collette threw in.

"Collette had a life-and-death experience of her own there," Dylan said.

Eve ceased the restless worrying of her coffee mug's handle. "What happened?"

"Explanation not fit for childhood consumption," Collette said, nodding toward Joey. "But the bottom line is, Dylan saved my life."

"Then she had to marry me," Dylan teased. "Collette's driving into the hospital a little later. You can wait and follow her in, Eve. That way Collette can introduce Joey to her favorite horses before you leave."

Eve hesitated before responding to the suggestion, but not long enough to convince Sean that she'd ever considered accepting his invitation to stay on at the ranch.

"Great idea," Eve said. "I'll follow Collette to the hospital and then be on my way. I'll get my things together as soon as I help clean up the kitchen."

Sean stared at Eve. Her shoulders were straight, her face and eyes showing only minimal signs of the emotional upheaval that had her quaking in the hallway mere hours ago. Only the tight muscles in her neck and her nervous fidgeting gave her away.

"Sean and I will clean the kitchen," Dylan said. "You three go out and enjoy the morning on the ranch. Joey, if you ask just right, Collette might even take you for a ride on Starlight."

Sean should let it go at that. Troubled horses were his forte, not stubborn, scared women.

He stood and gathered a few dishes to carry to the sink. Eve gathered the serving platters. When she left to go back to her bedroom, Joey, as always, tagged along beside her. The two of them on their own, about to go on the run again.

Sean waited until she was out of earshot. He could kick himself for what he was about to do, but he did it anyway. "I hate to disappoint you, bro, but I'm driving Eve to the hospital. Not to fear, though. I'll be certain you're there for the father/prodigal son moment."

Dylan looked puzzled. "Am I missing something here? Eve just said she would follow Collette in."

"She still will. I'll just be with her."

Dylan rubbed his freshly shaved chin. "Something tells me that knife removal routine must have been even more intriguing than it sounded."

"Let's just say it was eye-opening. It's mere suspicion at this point, but I think the shapely angel who came to our father's rescue last night might be in some trouble of her own."

"That would explain Dad's reaction to her visit," Dylan said.

"Interesting that Dad would know of her trouble, since it sounds like they haven't been in touch in years," Sean commented.

"Perhaps they have a mutual friend."

"Could be."

Dylan squirted some liquid detergent into the sink and turned on the water. "Just be careful. Good-looking women and trouble are a recipe for disaster."

Sean gave his brother a playful punch to the arm. "Who would know that better than you?"

"Exactly. So, on second thought, forget everything I said and go with your instincts."

Sean left his brother with the dishes and went off in search of Eve. He found her in the bedroom, zipping the overnight bag she'd thrown onto the bed and engrossed in conversation with Collette and Joey.

"Can my momma go with us?" the boy asked Collette.

"You don't need me to go see the horses," Eve encouraged. "You could go with Collette and I could pack, load the car and be ready to go when you get back. And, Collette, I'd rather he not ride one of the horses this trip. He's had no experience."

"Whatever you say," Collette said, "but

Starlight's extremely gentle, and I would have let him ride with me. I'd never let him do something dangerous."

Joey climbed onto the bed and scooted close to Eve. "What if we get lost and Momma can't find us?"

Collette sat down on the edge of the bed next to Joey. "I promise we won't get lost. I live here and I take care of the horses every day. That's my job on the ranch."

"Do horses bite?"

"Don't worry. I'll only introduce you to the friendly horses. I'll make certain they don't bite you," Collette assured him.

"You're such a big boy that you don't need me to have fun," Eve urged her son.

Joey looked as if he was being forced to choose between a stomachache and a smashed toe.

The kid reminded Sean of himself years ago. After his mother died and Troy went to prison, he'd suffered severe anxiety attacks. It had taken him years to get beyond them. And there really was no reason Eve had to be in that big a hurry to leave the ranch.

"I'd like to see those horses, too," Sean said. "Why don't the four of us just march down to that barn together?"

Joey grinned as if he'd just been offered gummy bears for breakfast. Eve gave Sean a stay-out-of-this look.

Nonetheless, a few minutes later they were treading the worn path from the house to the horse barn and the fenced pasture beyond. To Sean's surprise, Joey walked next to him.

"Watch the mud," Eve cautioned Joey when they approached a low spot. "You only have one pair of shoes with you."

Tennis shoes, Sean noted. "You need a pair of boots," he said. "A cowboy can't be worried about a little mud."

"Yeah, Momma," Joey agreed. "Cowboys have to get muddy."

Sean stooped low. "Climb on my shoulders, pardner, and I'll give you a ride over the muck."

Joey looked to his mother for approval. When she nodded, he grinned again and climbed aboard. Sean had worn jackets that weighed more.

"Can I feed the horses?" Joey asked.

"Sure," Collette said. "Like I said, that's usually my job, but I can sure use some help. And once you feed them, they'll really love you."

"Horses treat most people well, as long as

you respect them and teach them what you expect from them," Sean said.

Even when he'd been Joey's age, Sean had loved horses, especially Sinbad. It had been storming the night he was foaled, the thunder so loud it had rattled the horse barn as if it were kindling.

Sean's mother had insisted Sean stay inside, but his father had changed her mind. "A boy should see his own horse come kicking into the world," Troy had said.

Old memories of life on the ranch attacked without warning, and a violent churning rumbled in Sean's gut. The images grew painfully vivid. His dad teaching him to ride. Sean playing with his brothers on sunny afternoons. Him sneaking his first smoke behind the woodshed.

Stealing his first kiss in a clump of bluebonnets just past the old corral. Penny Rich. He hadn't thought of her in years. She'd been fourteen, with long, blond hair and budding breasts. He'd been twelve, with braces.

That same spring, he'd broken his right leg while practicing his calf roping for the first local rodeo of the summer. His mother had rushed to him, a look of pure panic in her dark eyes. Mom. Always there.

Until she wasn't.

Sean's knees all but buckled beneath him as the memories intensified. The ache that he'd spent years burying suddenly felt like a suffocating noose around his neck.

He should have never come back to Texas.

Only two things kept him from leaving right now—a woman who needed his help whether she admitted it or not, and the young boy who desperately needed her alive and well.

JOEY CLIMBED ON THE SLATS of Starlight's stall. With a little encouragement from Collette, he reached over and gingerly ran his fingers through the mare's mane.

Eve watched in amazement. Joey's curiosity about the horses no doubt had a lot to do with his fervor, but still, this kind of engagement with strangers was an auspicious accomplishment for him.

Even more surprising was the way he'd climbed on Sean's shoulders. He'd even questioned where Sean had gone when he didn't enter the barn with them. This from a kid who was still wary of the postman.

Joey looked back at her to make sure she was still nearby. She waved and smiled.

"A budding cowboy. All he needs is a hat and a saddle."

She turned at Sean's voice. "I thought you'd deserted us."

"I needed a minute to wrap my head around being back at the ranch," he admitted.

Naturally he would. She'd been so caught up in her own problems, she hadn't given much thought to what this homecoming must be like for Sean.

He stepped over to the nearest stall, crooned a few words to a gorgeous roan and then turned back to her. "I need a ride to the hospital. Whenever you're ready to go, no hurry."

The statement caught her off guard. "Your brother wants you to ride with him."

"I told him to go ahead without me. I'll catch a ride back with him if need be. Is that a problem for you?"

"If this is because you're worried about me, you needn't be."

"It's not you I'm worried about." Sean raked his fingers through his thick, dark hair, only to have an unruly lock fall back over his forehead. "I just want to make sure you're not stealing the knives."

It was clear that Sean could see right through her and her flimsy lies. But why did he care?

More importantly, how was she going to convince him she didn't need his help, when his offer became more tempting by the minute?

But she'd have Joey as a chaperone on the drive into town. That would ensure she didn't give into any crazy urges. And once they got to the hospital, she'd make some excuse to leave without seeing Troy. Sean would take her for an ungrateful wench, but that was far better than having Troy ask her about Orson in front of the others, and dragging his whole family into her problems. At least it would be better for them.

Hopefully, it wouldn't be a major mistake for her.

ALYSSA COLEMAN PEEKED THROUGH a slit in the blinds and into the glaring sun outside the front window of her San Antonio apartment. The unmarked car pulled up right on schedule and two men got out.

She figured the taller one to be Detective Reagan Conner. He walked and looked like he'd sounded on the phone. Authoritative. No-nonsense. Tough as nails.

Still no match for her brother.

Both men stopped on the drive where her

son Nick was shooting baskets. Nick laughed at something they said and then preened a bit as he sank the next shot. She didn't have to worry about Nick telling them anything. He'd never heard of his uncle Orson. She planned to keep it that way.

She stepped to the door and opened it the minute the bell rang. The two men flashed police IDs and she invited them inside. She wasn't intimidated by them. They'd threaten, but they were saints compared to what she'd grown up around.

She had no idea where her brother was hiding out, but she knew he'd be in touch with her again. He needed something from her, and he knew she'd be too afraid not to do as he asked.

She'd like to help the detectives. She'd like to stop her brother before he killed again. She really would.

But she liked living, so the good detectives would have to rely on their investigative abilities.

SEAN SQUEEZED EVE'S duffel into the crammed trunk of her compact car. The contents looked more like Eve and Joey were off for an extended vacation, not a quick trip to visit friends as she'd indicated. The three suit-cases could simply indicate she was a clothes-horse, but there were also two large shopping bags of books and toys for Joey, and a boxed video gaming set.

He rearranged a few things and took the liberty of snooping. A large zippered carry-on bag shoved all the way to the back held used Christmas decorations. A stuffed reindeer, a dancing Santa, a set of musical bells and a child's wooden nativity set. Tomorrow was only December first.

His suspicions multiplied and his anxiety level soared. His first instincts that she was on the run held even more credence. Possibili-ties ran rampant through his mind. Was she dealing with a stalker? A spurned lover? An irate ex-husband?

Or had she broken the law? Did she even have custody of the kid? And who had called her this morning at dawn?

He put everything back in place and closed the trunk. She wasn't a troubled horse that he could lock up in a stable or fence in until he could figure out what was going on in her head. If she was hell-bent on leaving, there wasn't a lot he could do to stop her.

For all he knew, she might be meeting up

with some secret lover who was just dying to take care of her. But if that were the case, why had she been so distracted and nervous at breakfast? And even when she'd been watching Collette take Joey for a ride around the small corral, she'd practically jumped the fence when a rabbit had hopped out of the tall grass behind her.

Sean turned as the front door of the house slammed shut. Joey settled on the top step with his Game Boy and a juice box that Eve had evidently brought with them.

Fighting the growing frustration, Sean went back into the house to grab his hat and a glass of water. He stopped when he spotted Eve standing behind the sofa in the family room. Her fingers dug into the cushioned back of the couch, and her expression was grim.

A picture of a guy who looked like your average tattooed bodybuilder stared back at him from the TV. The picture disappeared and the station's anchorman appeared in its place.

"Escaped convict Orson Bastion is still on the loose and should be considered armed and dangerous. It is quite possible that his appearance has been altered.

"If you see him or someone you think might

be him, contact authorities immediately. Do not approach him on your own."

Orson Bastion. There had been lots of talk of him on Sean's truck radio yesterday. He'd escaped from the same institution where Troy had been held. Sean had wondered then if his father knew the man. Judging from the intensity of Eve's focus, he'd say she definitely knew the escapee.

He muttered a curse under his breath as the truth hit him like a blow to the gut.

Eve picked up the remote and turned off the TV. When she started to walk away, Sean blocked her path.

"We need to talk, Eve." And this time he'd settle for nothing less than the truth.

Chapter Six

"What's your connection to Orson Bastion?" Sean demanded.

"Keep your voice down, please. You'll upset Joey."

"Then start talking. And skip the lies."

She took a deep breath and exhaled slowly. "He was an inmate at one of the prisons where I worked as a therapist."

"The same one Troy was in," Sean acknowledged. "Were you his therapist?"

"That information would fall under doctor/patient privilege."

"What happened between you and Bastion?"

"Nothing happened."

"And yet seeing him on TV practically sent you into fright convulsions."

She looked away, avoiding eye contact. "Orson's a vicious, unrepentant killer. I just hate to think what he might resort to in order to escape capture."

An unrepentant killer, as compared to his father, who she evidently saw as repentant? Only, that wasn't the case. Troy had never admitted to killing Sean's mother, so there was no way he could have come across as repentant, unless Eve knew something Sean didn't.

"Look at me, Eve. I only want the truth. Why did you really come to Willow Creek Ranch last night?"

Eve raised her chin, but hugged her arms around her chest protectively. Shadows haunted the depths of her eyes, and her trying to be tough only made her appear that much more vulnerable. And made it that much more important that he get the truth from her.

"I've told you why I'm here, Sean. I was in the area. I thought it would be nice to surprise Troy with a visit and see how he's adjusting to his release."

"On the same day Orson Bastion was released from prison. Interesting timing."

"And at the same time Troy was having a heart attack," she reminded him. "At least my stopping in unannounced worked for Troy.

Now, can we just drop this and drive to the hospital?"

He shook his head. "Not until you stop feeding me bull."

"You have far more important things to worry about than me, Sean Ledger. Your father is in the hospital. That should take precedence over everything else for you."

He wasn't buying it. He couldn't. The fear he saw in Eve Worthington was too real. "Did you come to Troy for protection from Orson?"

"No. No, of course not," she murmured. "I don't need protection." Stress added a tremor of desperation to her voice. She unwound her arms from her chest and started to walk away.

Sean grabbed her arm. Awareness sizzled though him like the sputter of hot bacon grease. He hated the effect she had on him, but that couldn't influence what he had to do.

"Tell me the truth, Eve. If not for your sake, then for your son's. Is there some reason Orson Bastion would come after you?"

She shuddered and swayed as if she were losing her balance. He pulled her into the circle of his arms to steady her.

Eve sighed, but this time she didn't pull away. "Okay, Sean. You're not going to give up until I tell you the ugly truth, so here it is—I testified against Orson at his parole hearing." Once she started, the explanation tumbled out in a rush. "I believed that if he got out, he'd kill again and again. He swore he'd make me pay."

"So you *are* on the run from Orson Bastion."

"Yes. I know it's probably paranoid of me to think Orson Bastion would give me a thought when he's running for his own life. But Gordon Epps, the prison warden, called me yesterday and suggested I ask your father to let me stay on his ranch until Orson was returned to the prison."

"Why Troy?"

"Because Troy's a man you can count on. I know that and Gordon knows it. And Gordon believes that the Willow Creek Ranch is the last place Orson would expect me to be."

"Because Troy is a former inmate."

"Exactly."

"Why didn't you just go to the police for protection?"

"I called them. I didn't feel they were taking the threat Orson made against me seriously.

But it doesn't matter. I shouldn't have come here. I realize that now. Even if Troy were well, he doesn't need me and my problems when he's trying to get his own life back together."

"Showing up when you did likely saved Troy's life."

"And I'm glad for that, but his heart attack is all the more reason I can't ask him to let me stay here. I don't think I should even visit him in the hospital."

"Where do you plan to go?"

"I don't know. This has all become extremely complicated. I just know that I have to keep Joey safe."

"Where's Joey's father?"

"He died two years ago."

Sean decided not to ask for details. Knowing too much about her personal life would break down barriers that he needed to stay in place.

"You shouldn't have to face this alone, Eve."

"I don't have a lot of choices."

"You have one." His arm tightened about her waist, and his muscles hardened, along with his resolve not to let this become personal. "Stay at the ranch. You'll be safe here."

She pulled away. "That wouldn't be fair to you or Troy. The two of you need time to reconnect without worrying about me."

"The reconnecting bit will either happen or it won't. Whether you and Joey are here will have no bearing on it."

She took his hand. The touch surprised him and sent a new bundle of confusing emotions coursing through him.

"I appreciate the offer," she said. "More than you know. But suppose we're all wrong and Orson does show up here? You can't even imagine what this monster is capable of."

"I worked with horses considered unbreakable for three summers while I was at the university, Eve. Orson can't be tougher than some of the disturbed stallions I tackled. And I've been the top marksman three years running in my National Guard unit. I think I can handle Orson if he's fool enough to show up in Mustang Run."

Her hand relaxed in his. "Stay on the ranch," he coaxed. "Joey can get lots of fresh air and sunshine. You can sleep through the night without worrying about defending yourself with a kitchen knife."

"What about Dylan and Collette?"

"What about them?"

"Don't you think you should get their approval before bringing the possible target of a madman onto the ranch?"

"If they have a problem with it, I'll let you know, and we'll go somewhere else—together. Trust me with this, Eve. I won't abandon you and Joey."

"Why?" she whispered. "Why are you so determined to become my protector?"

"Because a man who'd turn his back on a woman and kid in trouble isn't really a man."

"You, Sean Ledger, are a lot more like your father than you may ever admit."

He seriously doubted that. "Does that mean you'll stay?"

"For now. I can't promise beyond that."

Not the guarantee he wanted, but he'd deal with that issue when the time came. Other issues couldn't wait. "Now that I know what's going on, I think we need to call off our visit to the hospital. No use to risk anyone recognizing you and linking you to Troy."

She stiffened. "See, it's happening already. I'm coming between you and your father."

"I haven't seen the man in seventeen years," Sean said. "A few more days can't make that much difference."

"He's had a heart attack. No matter the prognosis, he could have another one. And even if he doesn't, your visit will mean the world to him. I won't stand in the way of that."

"So, do you have a better idea?"

"Don't use my name in front of anyone at the hospital. And I'll only go this once."

Sean decided to choose his battles wisely with Eve. This one would hit low on the priority level. Even if Orson was reckless and downright stupid enough to still be in Texas, it was unlikely he'd be hanging around a busy hospital.

The fact that Eve was staying on at the ranch was victory enough for now. He'd passed the first hurdle of the day. The second was facing Troy Ledger. He had little hope it would turn out nearly as well.

THE LARGE DOUBLE DOORS to the hospital slid open and Sean, Eve and Joey stepped inside. Having Joey in the backseat of his double-cab pickup had put any talk of Orson off limits. An uneasy silence had settled between them, giving Sean far too much time to think.

He hadn't lied. He'd have offered to help any woman and kid in legitimate trouble, but his feelings of concern for Eve were all mixed up with his uncanny attraction to her. It was not the normal kind of attraction to a good-looking woman, but a sensual onslaught every time he was near her.

It was the knife incident, he decided. Adrenaline and testosterone had formed a formidable alliance when he'd pressed against her, roaring though him with the ferocity of a mad bull. He'd been conscious of her every curve, deliciously aware of her breasts and hips when they'd pushed against his strained muscles.

That had been the fuel that had originally fanned the attraction. It went beyond that now.

He watched her as she walked toward the elevator, hips swaying, shoulders squared, silky hair bouncing. Her hand was clasped with Joey's. She was the perfect mix of spunk and warmth, obstinate yet seductively vulnerable.

And he was going overboard here. She was a woman in trouble. He'd offered his protective services. That was it. Start thinking differently, and it would lead to nothing but trouble.

He and women didn't mix—at least not

for long. They wanted more than he had to give. He'd proved that twice before. Only a fool would jump into the path of a kicking horse.

Okay, so he was lousy with analogies, too.

Now that they were inside the hospital, even the temptation of Eve couldn't alleviate the anxiety generated by his inevitable confrontation with his father. Just as he'd promised, Sean had called ahead to alert Dylan of their arrival.

When they reached Troy's room, Dylan and Collette were waiting for them in the hallway. Dylan smiled in anticipation and the dread rolled in Sean's stomach.

Cold. Calculating. Brutal. A murderer.

Sean had heard those words and worse, used by his mother's family over and over through the years to describe Troy. The unmarried uncle who'd become Sean's guardian had hated Troy even more than his grandparents—if that was possible.

At some point, Sean had separated the Troy Ledger they talked about with such hate from the man he'd known as Dad. For all practical purposes, his father had died the day Sean gave up hope of Troy proving his innocence.

Could there be even a fragment of forgiveness inside Sean for the man inside Room 212?

"You guys go in first," Eve said. "Joey and I will wait here with Collette."

"But you'll go in later, won't you?" Dylan asked.

She nodded. "Just don't mention my name in front of any of the staff. I'm traveling incognito this visit."

Dylan looked puzzled.

"Just go with it," Sean said. "We'll explain later."

"I'll hold you to that." He clapped Sean on the back. "Now let's get this show on the road."

Eve stepped in close. "Just give Troy a chance, Sean."

Dylan pushed the door open and stepped inside.

"The moment of reckoning," Sean muttered for the second time in as many days. A moment he'd probably live to regret.

Troy looked up as Dylan walked into his room. "I thought you'd gone home. Ranch won't run itself while you're up here catering to me."

"I have somebody with me that I think you'd like to see."

Troy pushed himself up so that he sat higher in the bed, and waited, expecting it to be Eve Worthington that followed Dylan in. He hated for her to see him like this, but he needed to talk to her, what with that bastard Orson Bastion on the loose.

It wasn't Eve.

Troy stared at the visitor, sure the meds were playing a trick on his mind. He blinked rapidly, his chest as hard as a lump of red Texas clay.

"It's Sean, Dad. He got in last night."

"I know." The words came out like they'd been pushed across sand. "I recognize him from the picture you showed me." Troy wrapped the fingers of one hand around the bed's side rail and extended the other hand toward Sean. "Hello, son."

"Hi. It's been awhile." Sean took a few steps into the room, but ignored the offered hand.

The invisible gap that separated Troy from Sean became palpable. It was more than the years that separated them. It was all the talks they'd never had, the doubts and suspicions and the pain they should have worked through together.

But Sean was here. That was more than Troy had expected, maybe more than he deserved. "Dylan tells me you're a horse whisperer, one of the best in the business."

"I'm a trainer. I've had good luck with troubled horses. The whispering reputation isn't my choosing."

"You were always good with horses," Troy said.

The memories crashed down like blocks of ice, freezing time, weighing him down. His eyes began to sting, and Troy closed them, not wanting Sean to see this weaker side of him.

"Yeah. Horses seldom disappoint you."

"Remember Sinbad?" Troy said, ignoring the sarcasm. "He didn't like for anyone but you to ride him."

"Yeah. I remember Sinbad."

"Did you stop by the ranch?" Troy asked.

Sean nodded. "I spent the night there last night. Didn't have a chance to see much of it yet, but what I saw evidences the hard work you and Dylan have put in on it."

"Collette, too," Troy said. Talk of the ranch was easier for him. "She's a hard worker, that girl. And she loves working with the horses."

"All that and a great cook, too," Sean said.

"And gorgeous, with great taste in men," Dylan added, no doubt trying to ease the tension that filled the tiny room.

Troy shifted and tugged on the hospital gown that always seemed to bunch up in the most uncomfortable of places. "Dylan tells me you've never been to the post."

"No, but came close a couple of times," Sean admitted. "Escaped the noose before the marriage nuptials got underway."

"You'll know when the right woman comes along."

"I'm not looking."

Didn't matter. Troy hadn't been looking either, but once he'd met Helene, he'd have turned his life upside down to get her to marry him.

Dylan leaned on the foot rail. "The cardiologist doesn't want you to have too much company, Dad, so I'm going to duck out and let the two of you visit for a few minutes."

"Thanks, and you don't have to keep driving all the way up here to check on me. I'm going to be fine. Won't be much help at the ranch for a few weeks, but I'll get there."

"Then you'd best talk Sean into staying on a month or so. A little fence-fixing with the peons will help me out and do him good."

Sean pulled a chair next to the bed and settled into it. Troy hoped he wouldn't start asking a bunch of questions about the past. He'd go there with him someday, but he'd rather it not be today. He was weaker than he wanted his sons to know.

Sean raked his hair back from his forehead. Strange how much he looked like the kid Troy remembered when he did that.

Sean leaned in close. "What do you know about Orson Bastion?"

Sean was dead serious now, his face drawn into tight planes and angles. Any resemblance to the kid from seventeen years ago vanished.

"Why do you ask?" Troy asked.

"He escaped from the prison in Huntsville. I figured you might have known him."

"I knew him all right. For starters, Orson is smart, conniving, manipulative and cunning—with the black heart of a devil."

"Sounds as if you knew him well."

"Better than I wanted to."

"I hear Eve Worthington also knew him well."

Sean had whispered the name, as if he thought the walls might overhear. Even in Troy's weakened state, he juggled the fact and came up with the only sensible conclusion.

"I take it you met Eve. Was she still at the ranch when you arrived last night?"

"Yes to both questions. She says Orson Bastion threatened to kill her for testimony she gave at his parole hearing."

"Yeah, and I have no doubt that he meant it. Where is she now?"

"Just outside the room, with Dylan and Collette. Her son is with her."

"I'd like to see her."

"You will, but first we need to square away a few things. I've asked her and her son Joey to stay at the ranch until this psycho is captured—just to be on the safe side. I'll stay, too, of course."

"So you've offered to be her bodyguard?"

"I guess you could say that, though evidently she and Gordon Epps think she won't really need one as long as she's at the Willow Creek Ranch."

"That explains why she showed up last

night. And I agree. I don't suspect Orson would ever think to look for her there."

"I haven't had a chance to discuss this with Dylan," Sean said.

"Dylan will be fine with it. Collette will, too. She knows what it is to need protection from a madman. And if anyone deserves a break, it's Eve. She's a giver, like your—" Troy stopped himself. Better not to bring up Helene until he and Sean were on more solid footing with each other.

Yet there was something about Eve that reminded him of Helene. That was the reason he'd let down his guard with her, had talked to her at length about what losing Helene that way had done to him. He shared his heartbreak with Eve, when he'd never been able to discuss that with anyone else.

"I think it best if only the family knows that Eve and Joey are on the ranch," Sean said. "And I don't want you to mention her name to any of your friends or the hospital staff."

"I agree," Troy said. "But if Orson decides to track Eve down, he'll find a way to do it. The only thing that will stop him is a bullet. Just so you know what you're getting into."

"I can handle myself, and a gun."

"I never doubted it." But just in case, Troy

planned to be in between Sean and Orson if it came to that. He'd failed Helene. He wouldn't fail their son.

Which meant that he had no time to spend flat on his back in a hospital bed. He'd have to recover. Fast. Before Orson found a way to make good on his threat.

THE FEAR WAS DROPPING AWAY from Eve like needles falling from pine trees. It had been four days since Orson's escape, and no more deaths had been attributed to him. The police now believed he was in Mexico.

She hummed as she spread a glob of chocolate frosting over the top of her freshly baked cake. If Orson had moved on, that meant she was out of danger.

Which also meant she had no real reason to stay on at the ranch. So why wasn't she excited at the prospect of going back to Dallas?

She smoothed more frosting around the sides of the three layers. The cake looked good. The test would be in the tasting. It was the first time she'd ever made a cake from scratch. The recipe had come from the internet. She wasn't about to admit to Collette that her culinary talents were pretty much nonexistent.

Her repertoire consisted of grilled chicken or fish, a baked potato, salad and of course the perennial peanut butter and jelly sandwich. And an occasional pizza delivery.

Sean and Dylan on the other hand, were beef men. Ranching gave a cowboy an appetite, Dylan had claimed last night, when he and Sean had grilled huge sirloins for dinner. Even Joey's appetite had improved in the three days they'd been here, though he only picked at the peas, butterbeans, squash and other veggies that Collette cooked on a nightly basis.

Joey wandered in from the living room, where he'd been watching TV. "Is that for a birthday?"

"No. The cake is for a homecoming."

"What's that?" Joey dragged a chair to the counter and climbed into it, resting on his knees for a closer look at the cake.

"Do you remember Mr. Ledger?"

"Uh-huh. He was sick."

"Right, but he's feeling better now and he's coming home from the hospital this afternoon."

Joey looked upset. "This is Sean's house."

"No, Sean is Mr. Ledger's son, but he doesn't live here. He's only visiting, as we are. This is Mr. Ledger's house."

"He should stay at the hospital."

"He's a nice man, Joey. You'll like him."

"What if I don't?"

"You like Sean. I'm sure you'll like his dad."

Eve sensed the anxiety building in her son. His fear of strangers, especially men, made life almost overwhelming for him at times.

She smoothed the last bit of frosting. "Do you want to lick the spoon?"

"I guess."

Talk of Troy's homecoming had sucked the enthusiasm right out of him. She handed him the spoon and gave him a hug. "It's going to be fine, Joey. And we'll be going home soon."

She was about to set the empty frosting bowl in the sink when Sean swung through the kitchen door. He dropped a package on the counter beside Joey.

"Looks like you got mail, pardner."

Apprehension stole Eve's breath. No one should know Joey was here. She snatched the package away before Joey could open it.

"It's okay. Let him have it," Sean said, tapping his finger on the address label.

It had been mailed to Sean from a Western store in Austin. She released her wrestler's grip on the package and let Sean take it from her and give it back to Joey.

She should have known Sean wouldn't have blown their cover or given Joey anything that could prove dangerous. No wonder Sean had kept his distance from her the last few days. Fear and paranoia had turned her into an untrusting control freak.

Joey climbed out of the chair and took his gift to the kitchen table.

Sean pulled out his pocket knife, cut the tape and walked back to the counter. "Cake looks good."

"Thanks. Hopefully, it's also edible."

"I'm sure it will be. Chocolate cake is my favorite."

Now she *really* prayed it was edible.

Joey studied his package, turning it around at different angles, as if it were a puzzle he was trying to solve.

"Open it," she urged.

"Men like to take their time," Sean said. He reached for the frosting bowl, raked his finger along the edge, collecting a mouthful of the creamy confection.

He started to taste it, then poked the laden finger in her direction, stopping an inch from her lips.

Her pulse accelerated. She parted her lips and he slipped his finger inside her mouth, then she wrapped her lips around it and sucked.

The sweetness of the frosting was no match for the delicious tingling sensation that vibrated all the way down to her core.

She wanted to return the favor, but didn't trust herself to carry it off with the same nonchalance that Sean had. He returned his finger to the bowl, this time tasting the frosting himself.

Sean licked his lips appreciatively. "Wow. You have been holding out on us in the cooking department."

"Better hold the praise until you've tasted the cake."

He smiled and hooked his thumbs in the back pockets of his jeans. "Nothing topped with chocolate frosting can be bad."

A blush heated her cheeks as she walked over to the table where Joey had finally torn the paper from his package. He reached inside and pulled out a black felt Western hat, a miniature version of the one Sean wore.

Joey ran his fingers over the brim, making the full circle before plopping the hat on his head. He adjusted it the way he'd seen Sean do his. Then he pulled a shoe box from the package.

"Boots," he said, lifting the cover.

"For keeping your feet dry," Sean said.

Joey grinned as he took them out one at a time, holding them up and examining them as if he were an art dealer and they were expensive relics.

Satisfied that they were the real thing, he sat down with them in the middle of the floor and kicked off his tennis shoes. He struggled with getting his foot into the new leather.

Eve stooped to help him, but Sean took her arm and tugged her back to a standing position before she could lend a helping hand.

"I was just going to—"

Sean silenced her with a finger on his lips and a shake of the head. A few minutes later, Joey's feet were fitted snugly into his new boots and he was beaming in triumph and excitement. The hat was knocked askew as he stood, but he straightened it himself and swaggered around the room.

"I'm a cowboy," he said.

"You sure are," Eve said. "A very handsome cowboy."

Joey walked over to Sean with just a trace of his usual shyness. "Thank you."

"You bet, buddy." Sean high-fived him. "Want to go see what the horses think of your new gear?"

Joey looked back at Eve. "You come, too, Momma."

"I'd love to, but I think from the sound of that car in the driveway that Mr. Ledger has arrived."

The mood of the room switched from carefree to somber in less than a heartbeat. Joey took off his hat and put it on the table. Sean stiffened, his face drawn, as if waiting for a firing squad.

The man was amazing with Joey, but apparently he had no expertise at dealing with his own emotional issues. *That could explain,* Eve thought, *why a man as wickedly tantalizing as he was single.*

Nonetheless, Troy Ledger was home and it was long past time for the two men to deal with seventeen years of mistakes, regrets and a murder case that had stolen much of their lives.

And time for her to get out of their way.

THE NIGHT WAS PITCH-BLACK, the light from the moon and stars blocked by layers of clouds that promised rain by morning. Orson

Bastion hunched behind the lonesome tomb-stone, waiting to make certain there was no one around to see him when he said his final farewell.

The branches in an old oak tree a few feet away creaked and groaned as they swayed in the wind. A funeral dirge that never quit. A sentry to watch over the legions of bones that would never rattle again.

Unsurprisingly, he was the only one at this forsaken cemetery in the wee hours before dawn. No one was following him. He'd out-smarted them all. It was exhilarating how easy that was to do.

Orson crept from behind the tombstone and walked the few steps to the grave of Lydia Bastion. Died at the young age of fifty-eight. She'd been only eighteen when he was born.

She was the only woman he'd ever loved, yet he hadn't been there when she put a gun to her head and pulled the trigger. Alyssa said her brains had been scattered about the garage like confetti.

He dropped to his knees and dipped his head until the top of it kissed the grassy earth. "Goodbye, Mother. I'm sorry that I wasn't the boy you wanted me to be. You loved me, anyway. No matter what I did, you loved me."

Drops of rain began to fall as Orson walked away from the grave for the last time. He climbed the fence and made his way to the nondescript black compact car he'd left in a patch of overgrown shrubs.

Reaching beneath his shirt, he touched the butt of the pistol in his shoulder holster. Most of the guys he'd met in prison liked heavy-duty arms. A pistol and a razor-sharp hunting knife were all Orson had ever needed.

That and his strength. He could squash a man with his foot or break a neck with his bare hands. Tonight all he'd need was the pistol. He'd done his research well. There would be no screwup.

Anticipation rocked though him. He started the engine and pulled onto the road.

Just a few more scores to settle. Revenge would be quick and sweet. And then he'd disappear south of the border for good. A free man, living the life he deserved.

Chapter Seven

Eve woke to the distant rumble of thunder. The room was dark and the house possessed an eerie predawn stillness that crept under her skin. A chilly draft passed over her, as if a cool hand had brushed her skin. For a second she imagined someone in the room, silently watching her.

She sat up straight, and the sensation passed as soon as she comforted herself with the sound of Joey's rhythmic breathing. Still, pinpricks of apprehension stung along her nerve endings.

In the bright light of day, she could almost convince herself that Orson Bastion was truly out of the country and out of her life for good. But here in the shadowed darkness, reality merged with memories, and if she let herself, she knew she'd sink into the past, into the horror that she didn't like to think about and never talked about.

Moving as quietly as she could, she threw her feet over the side of the bed and slid them into her slippers. Stealing from the room, she stepped into the long hallway.

Sean was just across the hall, and the door to his room was ajar. She hesitated, listening to his breathing, thinking of his body stretched out in the double bed. She wondered what he'd say if she took the initiative and crawled in beside him and curled her body around his.

Her good sense checked in quickly. He'd think she was nuts—or desperate. The latter probably wouldn't be that far off base. It had been two years since Brock's death, months more since she'd slept in the arms of a man. Not that she'd given her lack of sexual satisfaction that much thought until now.

Which meant this was merely a situational attraction evoked by Sean's status as a protector. Her reaction to him would level off as soon as she felt safe and secure, and the proximity issue no longer applied. Any decent psychiatrist would come to that same conclusion.

Unfortunately, resorting to psychiatric labeling and self-diagnosis didn't erase thoughts of Sean stretched out on his bed. Eve tiptoed down the hallway for a glass of cool water that would soothe her throat and hopefully tone down the unwanted desire.

When she reached the family room, the front door was slightly ajar. Her heart slammed against her chest.

"Is that you, Eve?"

Troy. She sighed in relief, thankful that she hadn't gone for a knife to attack a man in his own house for the second time this week.

"It's me." She went to the kitchen, filled a glass with water from the tap and joined him on the porch, closing the door behind her. "How did you know it was me?"

"Years of nothing to do but listen to approaching footfalls. The monotony of prison life fosters a multitude of useless skills."

"I suppose. Are you feeling okay?"

"A little tired. That's it."

"But you were having trouble sleeping?"

"I always do. I see the sun come up lots of mornings from this same spot. But that's okay. I love the freedom of just walking out that door anytime I choose."

"Seventeen years of paying for a crime you didn't commit, but it's all behind you now, Troy."

Troy dropped to the top step and stretched his long legs out in front of him. "Not everyone is as certain of my innocence as you are."

She leaned against the support post. "Are you talking about Sean?"

"Him, and others. He's the one most on my mind now."

Eve hadn't gotten the chance to visit with Troy alone this afternoon. Dylan and Collette had stayed through an early dinner, and then Troy had gone back to the master bedroom to rest. She hadn't wanted to disturb him.

Sean had barely spoken to his father, except to ask a few questions about the ranch. The strain between them had added layers of tension to what should have been a restful continuation of Troy's recovery. She was certain having her and Joey there for protection from an escaped convict hadn't helped either.

So, even if it came during the wee hours of the morning, she was glad to have this time alone with Troy.

"Sean just needs time to get to know you," she said. "He has years of indoctrination about your guilt to put behind him. He's here, and that's what's important."

"His staying has little to do with me. Not

that I'm not grateful he had the good sense to stop you from running off on your own. I sure didn't need to have to go looking for you in my weakened condition. Nonetheless, he'd be on his way by now if it weren't for you."

"Did he tell you that?"

"Not in so many words, but I see it in his eyes and in the way he backs out of a conversation with me before it gets going. I don't blame him. I should have pulled myself from the crushing grief and battled harder to prove my innocence. I should never have given up trying to contact my sons just because Helene's family fought me on it."

"Are you still obsessed with finding Helene's killer?"

"I don't think of it as an obsession, but yes. It's what kept me going all those miserable years in the pen. Her killer not only took her life years too soon, he stole her from me and from our sons.

"And for what? The few dollars we had in the house or to satisfy some inner demon? I'll never rest until I find him and see that he pays."

Eve dropped down beside Troy and put her hand on his arm. "You truly loved her, didn't you?"

"I still do." The words were all but swallowed by his pain.

Eve had difficulty comprehending a love that strong. "You must have been true soul mates."

Troy managed a smile. "Not unless 'soul mates' means opposites. We were nothing alike. She came from an influential, wealthy family. I was a loner who worked enough odd jobs to pick up entry money for the rodeo. She had class, read poetry, always had fresh flowers and scented candles in the house.

"I lived in worn jeans and dusty boots, drank beer from the bottle and thought there should always be a fiddle in the band. But I swear, I was so in love with her that even after five sons it was sometimes dizzying just to watch her walk into a room."

"Those are the things you should tell Sean."

"He'd still believe what he wants to believe. Everyone does."

Thunder rattled though the clouds and the first large drops of rain began to pelt the walk. It was the same weather they'd had on her last night in Dallas. The night before fear had sent her running to Troy and indirectly to Sean.

"Rain's setting in," Troy said. "I say we try

to get a few more hours sleep before the day starts in earnest."

They walked back into the house together. Troy closed and locked the door while she started down the hall.

"I'll be right behind you," Troy said. "I just need a glass of water to take another dadblamed pill. Hand me your empty glass and I'll put it in the sink for you."

"Thanks."

A few steps later, she heard whispering. Joey. And Sean. Joey must have wakened while she was on the porch. He'd probably called for her and she hadn't heard him.

She paused in eavesdropping range.

"I've had nightmares, too," Sean said. "In this very room. This is where I slept when I was a kid."

"Did you call for your mother?"

"Sometimes."

"What did she tell you?"

"That the dark was a cuddly black blanket that God gave the world so that we can sleep. Otherwise little boys would never want to go to bed."

"Did she hug you?"

"Yep. She was the best hugger in the whole world."

"My momma's a good hugger, too."

"I'll bet."

Eve was spellbound by the scene their words created. There were so many sides to this hunk of a cowboy who could tame wild stallions and comfort small boys.

She could come with all the psychological theories she wanted, but if she didn't leave here soon, she was going to fall hopelessly in love with him.

Both Joey and Sean looked up as she stepped into the room.

"Where did you go, Momma? I called you, but you didn't come."

"I'm sorry, sweetie. I stepped onto the front porch with Mr. Ledger for a breath of fresh air, and I didn't hear you."

"Sounds cozy," Sean said.

If the idea wasn't so ludicrous, she'd have sworn there was a tinge of jealousy in his tone.

Joey scratched his big toe. "It's okay, Momma. Sean heard me."

"I see." She was also bewitchingly aware that Sean was wearing nothing but partially zipped jeans that he'd probably grabbed and wiggled into at Joey's first call.

Joey reached for his stuffed lion that he'd

left at the edge of his pillow. "Me and Sean are cowboy buddies."

Eve pulled up the covers and tucked Joey in. "That's nice, cowboy, but I think you should go back to sleep now, so Sean can do the same."

"Okay. Thanks, Sean."

"You bet, buddy."

Eve gave Joey a peck on the cheek and then followed Sean into the hall and to the door to his bedroom. "You have quite a way with my son. It usually takes him much longer to warm up to a new man."

"Does he have to do that often?"

"It depends on where we go and who we run into."

Sean trailed a finger up the sleeve of her pajamas, letting it linger at her neck. "I was referring to your suitors. Do you date a lot of different men?"

"Me? None. I haven't been with anyone since my husband died."

His thumb rode her neck and tangled in her hair. "But you do like men?"

Her heart skipped crazily, leaving her positively giddy. "I like some men," she murmured, trying for nonchalance.

"Good."

His free arm encircled her, and he pulled her close. His eyes were dark and mesmerizing. His lips were dangerously close. "I didn't mean I like—"

Sean stopped her protestations with his lips on hers.

Eve closed her eyes and let the thrill of him zing through her. She was so lost in the moment that she'd totally forgotten about Troy still being up, until she heard his footsteps starting down the long hallway. Still, she felt cheated when Sean released his hold on her body and her lips.

"Sleep tight," he whispered, disappearing into his room before Troy reached them.

She stumbled to her door, stepped inside and leaned against the bed railing until she caught her breath.

Eve's heart was beating so erratically, she wondered if her pulse would ever return to normal again.

She wouldn't even try to analyze that.

WHEN EVE WOKE, the sun was beating through the window, the threatening storm of last night having moved on without ever fully developing. Eve knew that for a fact. She'd been awake for the intermittent rain.

Amazed and disturbed by the way an impetuous kiss affected her, she'd been unable to fall asleep for what seemed like hours. In a few weeks, she'd turn thirty-two. That was far too old for this type of infatuation with a man she barely knew.

Even with Brock, she'd insisted on moving slowly. Too many of her friends had gotten married in a fever, only to have the relationship cool down after the marriage. Her and Brock's relationship hadn't cooled down. It had run into an iceberg.

Joey was still asleep, though she knew that wouldn't last long. The clock said 8:15. Sean would likely be off somewhere on the ranch with Dylan by now. With Troy home, he surely wouldn't feel he had to stay so close.

She hoped Sean wasn't around. That was the problem with a kiss. It changed a relationship completely.

She shrugged into her robe, desperately needing that first cup of coffee. The enticing odor wafted down the hallway. So did the sounds from the TV. She tied her robe tightly and kept walking.

She heard the click of the remote as she reached the end of the hall. And then she saw

Sean, fully dressed, one boot on the hearth, his expression hard and strained.

"Is something wrong?" she asked.

"Sit down," he said. "I'll get you a cup of coffee." If his mannerisms hadn't said enough, his tone said the rest.

"Is it Troy? Did he have another attack?"

"Troy's fine. He had an early breakfast and went to his room to read the morning newspaper, fortunately without catching the morning news."

A shudder rocked through her. "It's Orson, isn't it?"

"Yeah. He's not in Mexico."

"Are they sure?"

"No absolute proof, but last night's murder has his name written all over it."

Eve collapsed onto the sofa, bracing herself for what would come next while Sean stepped into the kitchen. He came back with two cups of black coffee. He handed her one and dragged over a hassock, sitting on the edge so that he faced her up close and personal.

She took a sip of the coffee, needing the restorative power it usually provided. This time it lacked that effect. "What happened?" she finally asked.

"According to the news, the homicide

detective who had originally cracked the case and arrested Orson Bastion for the brutal beating death of his stepbrother was murdered at his home last night. Police are speculating that Orson is behind the murder."

"Was it a shooting?"

"No. I'm guessing a simple gunshot wound to the head is not Orson's style. The detective was stabbed repeatedly before finally having his jugular sliced."

"I'm not speculating," Eve said. "Orson killed him. I'm sure he did."

"If he's guilty of everything they say, that brings his total for the current killing spree up to three," Sean said. "The prison guard, the woman whose car he stole and now the detective. You were right to fight his early parole."

"We'll never know for sure. Maybe if he'd gotten that break, his anger might have diffused."

"Don't waste time second-guessing yourself with that monster. Men like that don't change just because someone does them a favor. You made the right decision. It's the system that made a mistake in letting him escape."

Being right gave her no pleasure and certainly no reassurance.

Sean curled his hands into fists. "Frankly, I'm tired of sitting around waiting for the bastard to make a mistake."

His vehemence worried her. "What does that mean?"

"Just what I said. All the police seem to do is wait for Orson to attack again. That's not my style."

"This isn't your fight, and you're not a cop."

"It's my fight if I make it my fight, and as for the police, they don't seem to be getting anywhere."

"What do you think you can do?"

"I want to learn everything I can about Orson Bastion. The more I know, the better chance I have of figuring out his next move before he makes it."

"He's not one of the horses you're used to working with, Sean. You can't micromanage him with theory. I know. I'm the psychiatrist here."

"Your being his psychiatrist is one of the things that will help make this work. I want to know all you know about this man, and don't give me that client privilege crap. If he represents a danger to himself or others, you can talk. So start talking."

This was happening too fast. She hadn't even had a chance to digest the latest gruesome crime. But Sean was right about the law. If the patient was deemed an imminent threat to himself or others, the rules of confidentiality didn't apply.

Orson Bastion wouldn't be worried about his privileges. His actions guaranteed that, if he was recaptured now, he would live the rest of his life in prison. She was certain he had no intention of going back to that life.

Not that Orson had ever leveled with her about anything when he was in therapy. He'd played mind games, said what he thought she wanted to hear. He'd known she was hired by the state to assess him, and he expected her to give him a glowing recommendation for early parole.

What she knew about the evil that festered inside Orson came from her own intuition rather than what he'd actually said. And from what other inmates had said about his cruelty when he was sure no guards were around.

She sipped her coffee and then placed the mug on the table beside her. "I don't know where to start."

Sean reached over and took her hands in

his. "Tell me what made you so sure that given the chance Orson would kill again."

SEAN WAS A SEETHING BUNDLE of nerves since hearing the news of last night's murder. It was clearly a revenge killing by a man who'd gone over the edge. Successfully taking out the detective exponentially increased the chance that he'd come after Eve.

Sean had no intention of letting the psycho anywhere near the ranch or her.

"I should start at the beginning," Eve said.

Sean got the impression that she was putting off the worst of her explanation, but there was time. He wouldn't push as long as he felt she was giving him the truth.

"When you counseled Orson, did you see him in his cell?"

"No, I saw him in a room designated for that purpose. There was always an armed guard right outside the room whenever I was working professionally with a subject."

"Did you see all the inmates?"

"No. I was hired by the prison to specifically conduct assessments, usually before prisoners were given more freedom within the institution or when they were up for parole.

Occasionally, I was asked to assess and make recommendations for prisoners who were considered at risk for suicide."

"How many times did you see Orson?"

"Probably a dozen or more."

"Sounds like a thorough assessment."

"Orson and a few other convicts, including Troy, were part of a one-time, special study I conducted to determine the effects of prison life on the morale of convicts who were serving sentences of over ten years."

So that's how she'd become such good friends with his father. Ironic, that the study involved a prisoner who made her fear for her life and another whom she'd come to for protection.

"So what made Orson different?"

"The way he talked about the murder that had sent him to prison."

"What kind of things did he say?"

"He blamed everything on his stepbrother, said he'd intentionally driven him over the edge. Orson claimed he hadn't meant to hurt the guy and yet it was reportedly one of the goriest crimes ever committed in that county."

"How long did he serve before he was up for early parole?

"Ten years and a few months. He was convicted of murder two because his defense attorney convinced the jury that his rage was linked to a drug he was taking for migraines."

"Exactly how did he kill his stepbrother?"

"He was waiting for the man when he got home from work that night. He beat him to death with the jack from his wrecked car. Pictures from the crime scene were so gory that two of the jurors got sick and had to leave the room after viewing only a few of them. The judge declared the prosecutor had shown enough to make his point."

Eve clutched her stomach as if thinking of the pictures was making her sick as well.

"Did you see the photographs?"

"Yes, and the images will haunt my mind forever."

And Sean was insisting she dredge it all up again. "That's enough for the time being."

"There's more you should know," Eve said, "and I'd just as soon get it all out now."

He got up from the hassock and sat beside her on the couch. He'd sworn after last night's kiss that he'd keep a safe physical distance between them, but this morning's developments voided those vows.

He snaked an arm around her shoulders.

Eve shifted so that she could see his face, but didn't move away from his touch. "Three weeks after Orson's failed parole hearing, he tried to kill me."

Fury burrowed inside Sean. Was there no end to the misery this man had caused her? "Where were the guards when this happened?"

"Who knows? Orson had been playing the system, had been a model prisoner in the months leading up to the parole hearing, had even claimed to have found religion. As a result, he'd been made a trustee. That offered him a lot more freedom inside the walled area."

Her shoulders tensed and Sean could only imagine the horror creeping back into her consciousness.

"I had finished for the day and was walking back toward my office, my mind already on the upcoming weekend and a planned trip to the zoo with Joey. Orson stepped out from nowhere and planted his meaty hand over my mouth before I had a chance to call for help. He dragged me into a small recreation room that was no longer in use and locked the door behind us. I managed to get in one swift knee to the groin before he slammed my head against the wall so hard that I lost consciousness. When I came to, he'd ripped all the clothes from my body."

Sean's muscles tightened as if wound with girded steel. "The son of a bitch."

"He didn't rape me," she added quickly, "but I'm sure that was his plan."

"What stopped him?"

"A prison work crew returning to the cells passed by and one of the inmates caught a glimpse of Orson through the window. I got out my one and only scream seconds later when Orson kicked me in the stomach.

"An inmate bolted from his group and smashed a fist though one of the window-panes. Instead of giving up and running away, Orson tightened his hands around my neck and squeezed. With his strength, he would have easily broken my neck had the inmate not managed to open the broken window and come flying at him."

Eve turned to face him and rested her hand on his thigh. "Your father was that inmate, Sean. Knowing the guard might shoot him for bolting and running, he still came to my rescue. Not even knowing who had screamed, he risked his life to save the victim. The jagged scar on his face came from a shard of broken window glass."

For years Sean had heard nothing but horror stories of how his father had brutally murdered his mother rather than lose her. Now he tried to wrap his mind around Troy as a brave prisoner willing to risk his life for a stranger.

The confusing images refused to jell.

Yet, if Troy hadn't gone to Eve's rescue that day...

The clunking sound of stamping footfalls shook him back to the present. He stood as Joey swaggered into the room, rubbing the dregs of sleep from his eyes with his little fists. He was still in his pajamas, but he was wearing his new boots and hat.

"Am I too late to help feed the horses?"

"You might be," Eve said.

"You shoulda woke me up."

"I have an even better idea," Troy said. "Why don't we take a trail ride on the horses and rustle us up a Texas cowboy breakfast."

Joey smiled and crawled up on the couch, taking the spot next to his mother that Sean had just vacated. "What's a cowboy breakfast?"

"You'll have to wait and see."

"Can Momma go, too?"

"I don't know," Sean said. "Can she cook?"

Joey shook his head. "Not cowboy food."

"Oh, well, I suppose we can take her with us anyway." As if he'd ever had any thought of leaving her behind.

"Mighty thoughtful of you hombres," Eve said as she gave her son a quick hug.

She smiled for the first time this morning, and the simple gesture lit up the room. Sean would do what he had to in order to keep her and Joey safe. That was a given.

Losing his heart would be a risk he'd just have to take.

Chapter Eight

Eve should have had zero appetite after news of the detective's murder. But cooking over an open fire after a brisk gallop to Willow Creek had left her famished. And thanks to Dylan and Collette, the task of cooking had been an easy one.

Dylan had delivered in his truck all the food and cooking equipment they'd needed, and had it waiting when they'd arrived at the perfect picnic spot. Their new house was only a hundred yards or so downstream and just over a slight ridge. Sean had pointed out the roofline before they dismounted.

Her stomach growled as the odors teased and tantalized her tastebuds. She spooned the spicy concoction of chorizo, scrambled eggs, melted cheese and salsa onto the fried tortillas, while Sean poured hot coffee for them and milk from a thermos for Joey.

Joey looked a bit dubious when she handed him his plate. "Is this really what cowboys eat?"

"When they can get it," Sean said, "especially if they can eat it outside on a brisk morning."

"What's brisk?"

"Cool weather, when you need a light jacket like you have on right now," Eve said.

She knew her son might not touch his trail-ride breakfast, but he'd loved the ride over the rolling hills and down the wooded trail to the creek. He'd ridden with Sean on a majestic quarter horse named Gunner. She'd ridden Starlight. The gentle mare was a good choice, since it had been years since Eve had been horseback riding.

Fresh air, the sound of Joey's innocent laughter, and the beauty of the countryside had been the perfect antidote for the dark mood that she'd been drowning in earlier. Not that it had changed everything. Danger was still waiting around the next bend.

Sean spread a blanket on the grass, a few feet from the muddy creek bank. Eve straightened the back corners before sitting down on it, taco and coffee in hand.

Sean joined her, sitting far enough away

that there would be no incidental brush of arms or shoulders. She wondered if that were an intentional decision so that she'd realize last night's kiss was no more than a natural reaction to a sensual moment. Or maybe he'd never given the kiss another thought.

Joey wandered toward a log that stretched to the water's edge.

"Watch where you're walking, Joey. It's muddy there."

From the corner of her eye she noticed Sean wince, as if she'd done something wrong. But she was only looking out for her son.

Joey turned back to her. "But I've got my boots on." He waited to see if she'd change her mind.

"Right." She gave in. "You've got your boots on."

Joey grinned and marched right through the deepest mud, on his way to the inviting log. He straddled it and set his paper plate on a dry spot near his feet.

"I'm not always this protective," she said to Sean. "At least I don't think I am. It's just that this ordeal with Orson has me too anxious to think straight."

"That's understandable."

"But you still think I need to give Joey more freedom."

"You're the expert."

"My friend Miriam thinks I hover over him. But his anxiety is real. A mother should protect her son."

"I'm not arguing with you."

Nevertheless, she knew he agreed with Miriam. Eve bit into her taco and the flavors exploded in her mouth. "Wow. This really is good."

Conversation ceased while she finished her breakfast. By the time she had, Sean had gone back for seconds. Joey, on the other hand, had pulled all the ingredients from his tortilla shell except a few bites of scrambled egg. The rest he'd tossed into the trees where a couple of black crows were noisily devouring the scraps.

Eve lay back on the blanket, the back of her head cradled in her hands, her eyes feasting on Sean. He was as hot a guy as she'd ever seen, but he was far more than the sum of his physical attributes.

"How is it you know so much about kids?" she asked.

"I used to be one. Besides, if you're talking

about the mud thing, guys of every age like riding horses and getting dirty."

"You'd make a great father. Why is it you never married?"

"Long-term relationships lead to complications."

"And you like your life simple?"

"Doesn't everyone?"

"Marriage works for some people. Look how happy Dylan and Collette are."

"Is this a proposal?" he teased.

"I was just making a point," she said, turning away so that he couldn't see the blush that was burning her cheeks. "And you didn't answer my question."

"I guess I just like doing things I'm good at."

Right now, Eve couldn't imagine anything Sean wouldn't be good at.

He finished his taco, set his plate aside and leaned back, propping himself up with an elbow. She looked into his dark, piercing eyes and her thoughts strayed into dangerous, erotic territory.

Wrong place. Wrong time. How could she feel even the slightest surge of passion after news of last night's murder? Yet her mouth ached to feel his lips on hers again.

Perhaps the latest research studies had been correct. Danger was a powerful aphrodisiac.

Her cell phone rang, destroying the moment. She checked her phone. "It's Gordon Epps."

"Probably just wants to make certain you heard the morning news."

Minutes later, any lingering feelings of desire vanished down the dreaded rabbit hole of more bad news. She was sitting up straight now, her resolve to remain calm pushed to the limits.

"Gordon heard from Detective Reagan Conner again," she whispered so Joey wouldn't hear. "This time he said it's urgent that I contact him. It's a matter of life and death."

Sean took her hand in his. "Anything to do with Orson Bastion is a matter of life and death."

ONCE THEY ARRIVED BACK at the house, the tension quickly swelled to volatile proportions. Fortunately, Collette was there visiting with Troy and she lured Joey to the protected courtyard garden on the pretense of needing his help in hanging some Christmas lights.

Eve insisted that Troy join them in the kitchen for the heated discussion.

"Homicide detective or not, he's still just a cop in my book," Sean protested. "If you let him know where you are, there's no guarantee that information won't get leaked to the press."

Eve absently straightened the edge of the tablecloth with her fingers. "The press knows nothing about my connection with Orson Bastion."

"You can't count on that," Troy said, backing Sean. "Orson is the lead story on every local news channel. Reporters are digging into everything they can find about his life. I'll be surprised if my run-in with him doesn't make the news."

"All the more reason I need to contact him," she said. "Just not from the ranch. We'll have to call from somewhere outside the Mustang Run area, just in case he's able to track the call."

"He'll track the call," Troy said. "Count on it. That's why he gave Gordon a specific line for you to use when calling him."

"Cop or not, I don't think you should let Detective Conner know where you are," Sean insisted.

Eve stood and paced the floor.

Troy worried the scar at his temple. "Why

not call your brother, Wyatt, Sean? He'll have suggestions for how this should be handled."

Eve tried to remember what Troy might have told her about Wyatt. She drew a blank. The stress was getting to her.

"Wyatt's a homicide detective in Atlanta," Sean explained. "One of the best. And Troy's right. Wyatt will know how to handle this."

Eve wondered how Troy felt about Sean never calling him Dad. She shot him a look. If it bothered him, he gave no sign.

"I don't know why I didn't think of Wyatt first," Sean continued. "I'm betting he has access to an untraceable line, and he doesn't have to use the Ledger name."

"You can trust Wyatt," Troy assured Eve. "He won't do anything to give away your location. He definitely came through for Dylan when Collette was in danger."

"Then let's call him," Eve conceded.

She tapped her fingers against the wooden tabletop as Sean made the call. The easy phone camaraderie matched what Sean shared with Dylan. Troy was the odd man out. Her heart went out to him. Surely, given time, Sean would see that his father could never have killed his beloved Helene.

If not, they'd both be the loser.

WYATT ANSWERED ON the third ring. "If you're calling with trouble, hang up."

"That kind of day?" Sean asked.

"You know it. I'm thinking of chasing a job wrestling alligators. It would have to be easier. How's Troy?"

"Improving every day. But I need a favor."

"Sorry," Wyatt said. "I won't come down and rescue you from family life. You're on your own."

"This has to do with a woman."

"Even worse."

Sean gave Wyatt the scoop in as few words as possible.

Wyatt responded with a couple of well-chosen curse words. "First Dylan, now you. Are there any women in Texas who don't need protecting?"

"Probably, but I'm just concerned with the one now," Sean said. "Is there any way you can make that call to Reagan Conner without the Ledger name coming into play?"

"I can do better than that. I can connect Eve to him through a line that it will be impossible for him to trace or track the location of."

"The wonders of modern technology," Sean said.

"Yeah. Too bad the criminals can afford it

before we get it. Give me the number Conner said to use. I'll get him on the phone and then give you a call back at this number."

By the time Sean had explained the plan to Eve, the call came through. Sean took her hand and squeezed it. "Remember, I'm right here, and no matter what Conner says, I have your back."

Eve took the phone and identified herself to the detective.

"I'm glad you called, Mrs. Worthington. I've been trying to get in touch with you for several days. I've left countless messages on your phone."

"I'm out of town."

"I assumed that, but the department is concerned for your safety."

"The department didn't sound all that concerned when I contacted them the day after Orson Bastion escaped."

"I'm sorry for that misunderstanding, but under the present circumstances, I assure you that I'm prepared to offer you protection twenty-four seven, if you return to Dallas. I'll even send an escort to pick you up and drive you back here."

It didn't add up, Eve thought. Conner seemed too eager to help. "I appreciate your offer, but I prefer to take my chances on my own."

"That's not smart, Mrs. Worthington. Not for you or your son. I would have preferred not to frighten you with this, but you leave me no choice."

"No choice in what?" she asked, growing even more nervous.

"We have credible evidence that suggests that Orson Bastion may be planning to kill you."

Her stomach roiled. "What kind of evidence?"

"I can't reveal that, but like I said, it's from a credible source. I think you're in real danger. That's why we're willing to make certain you're protected if you return home."

"And suppose you can't?"

"We can do a better job than anyone you can hire for that purpose. And if you're working on the assumption that Bastion won't hunt you down wherever you are, you're putting yourself and everyone around you at extreme risk."

Everyone around her. Like Troy and Sean. She knew both of them would take on Bastion to save her and Joey, but at what cost?

"I'll consider your offer," she said.

"Think too long and Bastion may take it out of your hands."

Once the connection was broken, she filled Troy and Sean in on the details of the conversation. Sean became increasingly agitated.

Finally, he slammed his right fist against the table. "The detective isn't worried about you, Eve. He just wants you back in Dallas to use you for bait. He'll have his men there twenty-four seven all right, but they'll be there to arrest Bastion when he shows up to kill you."

Which might be the only way to stop him, she realized. But there was a major drawback. "I can't risk exposing Joey to the danger or to the sight of violence."

"It's too risky for both of you," Sean said. "You're in the safest place you can be. And that's settled."

"It's *my* decision," she said, not sure why she was angry with him, except that he was taking over and that her emotions were so raw she was suddenly fighting back tears.

"Do you want to leave and go back to Dallas?" Troy asked.

"It's not a matter of what I want. If I stay, I'm dragging all of you into danger. I've known that all along, but hearing it from the detective makes it even more imperative that I leave the ranch."

"I don't take Bastion or his threat to kill you lightly, Eve." Troy propped his elbows on the table and waited until she met his gaze. "But I'm not afraid of him, either. You're not only welcome to stay here until he's apprehended, your being here would save me a lot of worry."

"I appreciate that."

Sean rolled his eyes, as if it irritated him that his father had played the situation a lot cooler than he had. He pushed back from the table. "So, are you staying here or running back to Dallas?"

She shook her head. "I need time to think."

Sean's phone rang again, no doubt Wyatt calling to check out the status. She slipped out of the room. She'd heard enough. Now she just wanted to see her son. He had to be protected at all costs, and she could not afford a mistake.

No matter what Troy, Wyatt, or even Sean thought, in the end, her son's safety was her responsibility. But if she could protect him and help in Bastion's apprehension, it would be a win-win for everyone.

"HOW ABOUT PASSING THOSE pork chops?"

"This sweet potato casserole is the best I've ever tasted."

"Glad you requested macaroni and cheese, Joey. I don't remember when I've had that last."

"Eve gets credit for that."

"And I did it without a box," Eve said.

Collette had invited them all for dinner, and conversation flowed like it might on any ordinary night. For Sean, though, it was anything but. Tension churned inside him. He hadn't spoken directly to Eve since the afternoon's phone call to Detective Conner. He couldn't even think straight, what with her considering going back to Dallas and marching right into the hands of a madman.

Wyatt had agreed with him that Eve was being set up as bait. He'd stressed that that didn't mean she wouldn't be protected. But setting a trap for Bastion would still put Eve's life on the line. Plans could be fouled, and even the best of cops made mistakes.

Sean could not let her go back to Dallas until Bastion was behind bars. Only, if she made up her mind to go back, how in the devil was he supposed to stop her? Kidnap her himself?

Maybe that wasn't such a bad idea.

He studied her across the table while she ate. Unlike him, she was engaging in conversation with the others, even smiling at times. But the dark circles around her eyes, the strain to her facial muscles, and even the stoop of her shoulders revealed that the growing threat of danger was weighing on her.

And still, he ached to just carry her off somewhere and...

And what? Finish what he'd started last night? Kiss her senseless? Make love to her?

All of the above, he silently admitted.

He was falling for Eve. Hard. Under normal circumstances, those feelings would likely have him running for his life. Who was he kidding? He had nothing to compare this to. He'd never felt like this about another woman. And that included the two he'd thought himself in love with.

Desire rode him hard and he looked away, determined to focus on the conversation and make it through this meal.

"How was that trail ride this morning?" Dylan asked.

"Awesome." Joey moved the casserole around with his fork. "But riding the horse with Sean was the best fun. And wearing my new boots. I got them real muddy, but Sean showed me how to clean them up."

And if Sean's agonizing over Eve wasn't enough to deal with, he had Joey to think about. Joey had lost his father. Losing his mother to a psycho killer would destroy him. Who knew that better than Sean?

Yet, here he was sitting at the same table with Troy Ledger. Troy wasn't the man Sean remembered running to as a kid. He wasn't the man who'd taught him to ride, played ball with him and his brothers on Sunday afternoons, let him jump from his shoulders at the swimming hole. He wasn't the man who'd stood beside him and told him it was okay to cry when his dog died from a rattlesnake bite.

Troy was older, hardened, and the easy laugh that Sean remembered never came.

But was he the man that Sean had heard about time after time over the last seventeen years? Was he a heartless, brutal killer who'd killed Sean's mother rather than let her escape the marriage?

Dylan was convinced that Troy was innocent. Sean might reach that same conclusion one day; but until he did, he couldn't just act as if the stranger at the table mattered in his life.

The truth was, he couldn't deal with Troy, Eve or family now. "Dinner was great," he said, "but if you guys will excuse me, I have a few things I need to take care of back at the house."

But before the night was over, he'd have to speak privately with Eve and talk some sense into her before it was too late.

"Take all the magazines you want," Collette urged. "I think there's even a few Hollywood gossip sheets in the mix, in case you want to know who's sleeping with whose ex."

"And lots of books on photography, I see," Eve said, picking one up and thumbing through it.

They were back in Collette's bedroom, looking for some fluff reading material. All Troy had at the house were ranching periodicals, and articles on winter feed for beef cattle read like a foreign language.

Not that she expected to really get her mind around any article tonight.

"Do you take a lot of pictures?"

"Constantly," Collette said. "That's what I

did for a living before I met Dylan. I kept my studio in town, but I mostly concentrate on creative imagery now, instead of weddings and parties. I still do family and personal photographs on occasion."

"Then you still work?"

"Yes, but mostly from the ranch. It makes a great natural setting for family photos. In fact, I have several appointments scheduled next week. Christmas brings out the need to preserve memories for posterity."

"I can't believe we're already in December."

"And the next few weeks will fly by. I just sprang for adorable Mr. and Mrs. Santa suits. You'd be surprised how many folks love the quirky for their Christmas card shots. You should dress up in one and let me take your picture with Joey, not that you'd even be recognizable in the wig and padding that go with it. Hey, we might even get Sean to pose in the Santa suit, as long he could wear his boots and cowboy hat."

"If we drugged him and tied him down first." Eve laughed in spite of the anxiety that never let up. But she was in no mood for Christmas photos. Orson and peace on earth, goodwill to men were not compatible. "How much do you know about my situation?" she asked.

"Everything Sean has told Dylan," Collette said. "My husband and I don't keep secrets from each other. Orson Bastion sounds beyond evil. I hope they capture him soon."

"So do I, but in the meantime, are you sure that you and Dylan are okay with me bringing my problems to your doorstep?"

"Absolutely. I brought mine here before you did. Dylan was a lifesaver in the most literal sense of the word. When things settle down for you, I'll share the gritty details. For now, just know you're in good hands with the Ledger men."

"But it was different for you and Dylan. You were in love. Sean barely knows me."

Collette dropped to the floor beside Eve and the basket of magazines. "Don't tell me you haven't noticed that Sean looks at you like you're a bowl of whipped cream that he's dying to dive into?"

A slow burn crept to Eve's cheeks. She hadn't noticed the way Sean looked at her, but if Collette had, then she'd surely noticed the way Sean affected her. Memories of last night's kiss vibrated through her.

It was positively insane for her to experience this kind of desire with all she had to face.

She picked up another magazine, only to find herself staring at a picture of the Ledger ranch house plastered across the cover.

Beyond the Grave

"Oops, forgot that one was in there," Collette said. "Ignore it. It's all hype and hyperbole anyway. And not good bedtime reading for you right now."

But Eve couldn't bring herself to return *Beyond the Grave* to the stack. She thumbed through it until she found the cover page story.

The opening lines made the hairs on the back of Eve's neck stand on end.

"Does the ghost of the wife of Troy Ledger still inhabit the house where she was brutally murdered? Does she still walk halls at night, looking for her sons so that she can tuck them into their beds? Or is she there waiting on her killer to return?"

"Who wrote this?" Eve said. "And why?"

"It's nothing," Collette said. "Really. Pay the article no mind. The editors of the publication are friends of mine. Sounds weird, I know, but they're great gals who just happen to believe in the paranormal and in making a living from it."

"Did you take the pictures?"

"No, but as a favor to me, Troy gave them permission to take all the photos they wanted of the house and gardens and to do the story. They're really trying to make a go of the magazine, and the story on the Ledger house did give them a giant boost in sales."

Dylan tapped on the open door and stuck his head inside. Joey was a step behind him, holding on to a bag of wood scraps that Dylan had given him earlier to use as blocks.

"I'm going to drive Troy back to the house. I think that big construction project Joey had him working on wore him out."

Joey skipped over to where Eve was sitting cross-legged on the floor. "We used the blocks to build a ranch with a place to ride horses and everything," Joey said. "And we made a bridge to go over Willow Creek."

"So that's what's kept you quiet for so long?"

"I can drive you two home later if you want to visit a while longer," Dylan offered.

"No, I need to get Joey to bed, and I'm a bit tired myself. It's been a long day."

Eve grabbed the stack of magazines she'd

put aside, stood and started to the door with Joey a step behind.

Collette followed them out to the truck.

"Thanks for everything," Eve said as she climbed into the backseat with Joey.

"You're welcome. Come back tomorrow and I'll take some shots of you and Joey down by the creek. Maybe we can get one that's frame worthy."

A picture to take home with her to remind her of the week she'd spent on the run. Only, she wouldn't need a reminder.

If all went well and Bastion was caught and returned to prison, the terror would pass, she told herself. The heated memories of Sean would haunt her forever, especially if she never got to finish that kiss. Depending on the plan brewing in her mind, that might have to be tonight or never.

And never was much too long to wait.

Chapter Nine

Eve lay on her back in the twin bed, staring at the ceiling and feeling totally alone as she let the plan take shape in her mind.

The most difficult part would be leaving Joey at the ranch with Troy and Sean so that he'd not witness any violence. He'd be anxious with her away, but not as traumatized as if she'd left him before he'd developed a case of hero worship toward Sean. Sean might be furious at her for leaving, but she was certain he'd keep Joey safe.

She'd go back to Dallas alone. When Orson made his move, the police would arrest him. Orson would return to prison instead of continuing his killing rampage. And it would all happen without Joey being exposed to violence and without putting the Ledger family in danger.

Orson was likely already watching her

house, waiting for a chance to make good on his death threat. But he wouldn't show his hand until she was on the scene.

He'd rely on his intellect, have what he thought was a perfect plan to kill her without getting caught. Why wouldn't he feel confident? He'd killed three times since his escape. He carried no guilt. He had no conscience.

But this time Detective Reagan Conner and his team would be there waiting on him. They'd stop him before he could kill her, and then it would all be over.

Unless… Unless any one of a dozen things went wrong.

Suppose the police didn't act fast enough. Suppose Orson really was too cagey to be apprehended again.

One mistake and she could be dead, and Joey would be left without one living family member to take care of him.

Doubts expanded into new avenues of dread. Apprehension rattled inside her like a nest of venomous snakes. She knew what Sean's answer would be to the dilemma, but still the need to talk to him about it swelled to a painful ache.

Or maybe it wasn't talk she needed at all.

She touched her mouth, and anticipation heated her lips and curled around her fear.

She was trembling when she reached the door to Sean's bedroom. It was ajar as before. She tapped lightly.

No answer. No sound of his breathing. No sounds coming from his room at all. She stuck her head inside. The bed was still made. There was no sign of Sean.

She hadn't seen him since Dylan had driven them home, but his truck had been parked in the driveway at the side of the house. She'd assumed he was in his room. Obviously she'd been wrong.

Disappointment crept though her in fatiguing waves as she padded back to the bedroom she shared with Joey. Too unsettled to sleep and not wanting to wake Joey, she picked up the stack of magazines and carried them to the family room. The house was unsettlingly quiet as she flicked on a lamp and nestled into a corner of the leather sofa.

The journal on top was seriously out-of-date. She reached into the stack and made a random choice, not realizing what it was until she'd placed it in her lap.

Beyond the Grave. She hadn't intended to bring that one with her. A chill settled in the room as she thumbed through the magazine, found the article and began to read. If there were facts to be discovered, they were concealed in the darkly evocative narrative.

The Ledger house had a reputation as being haunted. Strangers told of seeing a woman in white out by the gate when they'd pass it at night. She'd try to wave them down as if she needed help. If they stopped, she disappeared.

Others who had dared venture inside the gate claimed to have seen a woman standing at one of the house's many windows. Speculation was that the woman in white was the ghost of Helene Ledger waiting for her five sons to come home. Others believed she was there to make sure that her husband never returned to the house where he'd killed her.

In all fairness, all the writers really attested to was that the house had a warm and welcoming feel to it and that Troy Ledger's new daughter-in-law was totally convinced of his innocence.

The article included several pictures of the courtyard garden that Collette and Joey had decorated for the upcoming holiday this afternoon. It was said to be Helene's creation and one of her favorite respites before her murder.

The garden had now been lovingly restored to its former beauty. If the ghost of Helene Ledger was still on the scene, the writers were certain her days would be spent there, even if she did roam the hallways at night.

Creepily grotesque, yet weirdly sentimental. Throw in a dollop of unrequited passion for a fascinating stranger and you'd have Eve's life in a nutshell.

She didn't believe in ghosts or goblins or any other paranormal elements. But her psychiatric training and experience had taught her that the mind could mold any fear or fantasy into a virtual reality.

If Helene's ghost were real, it would surely be furious with Eve for bringing danger into the Ledger home.

Her eyelids grew heavy. Eve reached for a nearby throw, pulled it over her and snuggled against the back of the couch. Her head came to rest on her folded arms, and the magazine dropped to the floor.

An icy draft filled the room. Eve shivered and opened her eyes as a strange, vaporous shape floated past her and hovered above Joey's bed. The vapor formed long, sinewy bands that wrapped around Joey like tentacles.

Eve rushed over and tried to beat them off him, but her efforts met with inhuman resistance.

"I'll watch over him. He's cradled in love."

Eve jerked awake as the words echoed in her mind as if they'd traveled through a deep canyon. A cold sweat dampened her pajamas and they clung to her like a second skin. She sat up straight and took gulping breaths to clear her mind.

There were no remnants of a ghostly vapor. She wasn't even in the bedroom where Joey was sleeping. But her conscience had found a way to get through the hurdles she'd erected in her mind.

Joey would be safe here at the ranch without her. She'd go back to Dallas. Detective Conner would get his man. Her world would return to normal.

Normal, but without Sean Ledger in it. She ached to go to him now, beg him to hold her until her nerves steadied.

But if he held her in his arms, she'd never find the strength or the will to leave him. That left nothing to do but go back to her own bed. Alone.

She'd tell Sean and Troy of her plans the first thing in the morning.

SEAN STAMPED THE MUD OFF his feet and climbed the back steps. He'd slept very little last night and woke up with the sun. Hating to disturb the others at that ungodly hour, he'd moved through the house as quietly as he could, made a pot of coffee, and taken a cup outside with him.

He'd taken a brisk walk, got his blood circulating and still dreaded the thought of stepping back inside the house. He and Troy had found no meeting of the minds. They hadn't even come close.

They wouldn't, as long as neither of them took the lead in bringing up his mother's murder. They sidestepped the subject like it was a cliff they'd fall over if they got too close.

Worse, he was losing it with Eve, letting his frustration turn him into a drill sergeant. But she wasn't helping any. She didn't have to look so damned irresistible or sway so seductively when she walked. Or return his kiss with a passion that left him dizzy with desire.

If he let himself, he'd fall so hard it would take a team of horses to right him. He'd even start believing he could actually make a relationship with her work, when experience had taught him it was a mistake to even try.

The only thing going well was his relationship with Joey. Sean could read Joey the way he read a troubled horse. The boy reacted honestly and without thinking about his every move. He wanted independence, yet his dependence on his mother got in the way of his claiming it.

What Sean couldn't decipher was exactly how or why Joey had become so fearful, though he knew a traumatic experience could do that to a kid.

Like coming home from school and finding your mother lying dead in the living room, her hair matted with blood. Sean pushed the gruesome memories back into the crevices of his mind as he stepped through the back door. He took off his Stetson and tossed it onto an empty chair.

Troy was sitting at the kitchen table, reading the morning newspaper and sipping his coffee. He nodded and kept reading.

Sean stared at the jagged scar that punctuated his face from his temple to his cheek and he recalled the story Eve had told him.

Troy was not the fallen hero from his youth. Nor was he the heartless monster his mother's family had claimed.

Sean refilled his coffee mug and joined Troy at the table. "Can we talk?"

TROY FOLDED THE PAPER and pushed it aside. He'd been expecting this ever since Sean had arrived. Still, he wasn't prepared. Explaining meant revisiting the pain.

It meant saying things that should never have to be said. It meant facing head-on the revulsion that Sean had never really tried to disguise.

"I guess now's as good a time as any for you to say what's on your mind," Troy said.

"Do you remember me?" Sean asked. "I mean really remember me and not just that I'm one of your sons that you dismissed from your life for seventeen years."

"I remember you. When I was around, you took every step I did until you started school. Even as a tyke you loved horses. I brought a saddle in the house and you'd sit in it and act like you were riding. 'Yee-haw' was practically the first word you said."

The first word had actually been "Momma." Troy's chest tightened at the memory. Sean was their second son. He'd been born just a year and a half after Wyatt.

It had been a difficult pregnancy for Helene. Not that she'd ever complained, though Troy had given her plenty of reason. He worked sunup to sundown trying to get the ranch up and running so that he could make enough money to pay the note on the land.

Ranching was all he knew. That and rodeo, and he couldn't afford a wife and kid on his rodeo winnings.

Helene was used to luxuries. With Troy she'd gotten calluses and kids. Her parents had never forgiven him for that. Troy figured this was not the kind of information Sean was interested in.

"You were a heck of a baseball player," Troy continued. "Your team won every game that last year...." The last year before Helene had died. Troy hadn't meant to go there, but it was out there now, hanging in the air, waiting to sting like an angry wasp.

Sean looked him straight on. "Did you kill Mother?"

The answer screamed inside Troy, but yelling it out loud wouldn't make much difference.

He'd told the truth from day one. People made facts of whatever they chose to believe.

"You must have made up your mind about my guilt or innocence a long time ago," Troy said.

"I had lots of help."

"From your mother's family?"

"And from a jury."

"I'm not going to knock your mother's family, Sean. They never approved of Helene marrying a poor rancher, but they loved her very much. And they stepped in and raised all of you boys when I couldn't. There's no way I could ever repay them for that, not that they'd want or take anything from me.

"As for the jury, I can't even really blame them for convicting me on circumstantial evidence. I didn't do a lot in my own defense. A big part of me died the day your mother did. I shut down mentally and emotionally."

Troy forced himself to look Sean in the eye, hoping for some sign of understanding, if not forgiveness. The stare he got in return was unrelenting.

"I let all of you boys down, Sean. I let Helene down. I can't change that now, but I'll never forgive myself. But for the record, I did try to get in touch with you through the years. Your grandparents convinced me that you didn't want to hear from me and that forcing myself on you would just make matters worse."

"They were right," Sean admitted. "I had never planned to see or talk to you again."

Yet here he was. Troy was thankful for even that.

"I'd like to believe every word you said," Sean said. "I'd like it more than you know. But just wanting to doesn't make that happen for me, not the way it happened for Dylan."

"It didn't happen that fast for Dylan, either. We went through some tough times. But I can't change any of the past."

If he could, Helene would walk through that door right now, and her smile would make his heart sing.

"Just don't let the past mess up your mind and keep you from finding happiness with someone you love," Troy said. "You don't have to take a chance on me, but take a chance on you."

The silence grew heavy, and Troy was thankful when it was broken by the ringing of Sean's cell phone. He'd said what he could. The rest was up to Sean.

He'd turned into a man's man. Good. Honest. Brave.

Helene would be proud of him.

And knowing what a matchmaker she was, she'd no doubt be pushing him into the arms of Eve Worthington right now. In fact, Troy kind of liked that idea himself.

He stepped out of the kitchen, leaving Sean privacy for his call.

"DID I WAKE YOU?" Wyatt asked.

"Unfortunately, no."

"A restless night?"

"And a worse morning. Tell me, Wyatt, do you think there's a chance that the whole lot of Mother's family misjudged Dad and that he really is innocent?"

"To tell you the truth, nothing seems black and white to me anymore. Dylan sees one shade of gray. You see another. Dakota and Tyler were so young back then, I'm not sure they remember enough to form a judgment."

"I know why Tyler hasn't come around. He's fighting in Afghanistan."

"And Dakota's chasing a championship buckle in the Canadian rodeo circuit," Wyatt said. "What's your point?"

"I was just wondering why you haven't made a visit to the Willow Creek Ranch."

"Doesn't rank at the top of my to-do list right now. I've got killers to get off the streets of Atlanta—not to mention the hottie model who either pushed or watched her prominent sugar daddy fall out of a penthouse window last night."

"Are we still talking about Troy, or is that your way of telling me that you were too busy to check out Orson Bastion?"

"I managed to dig up a few specifics. I'm just not sure they'll help you."

"Hit me with them."

"His mother's name was Lydia Cantrell, though she'd gone back to calling herself Lydia Bastion before her death. She killed herself a couple of years back, supposedly because of Orson's failed parole attempt."

"Was she married?"

"Not at the time. Her third husband, Sam Cantrell, left her after Orson beat his son to death with a carjack."

"Guess he figured the 'till death do us part' clause didn't extend to a son's murder as well," Sean said. "Does Orson have any living family?"

"A sister named Alyssa Coleman. Divorced.

One son, Nick, age eleven. She lives in San Antonio."

Wyatt read off the address and Sean scrawled it on a napkin he grabbed from the kitchen counter, though he was certain Orson wouldn't be hanging out there.

"Where does Alyssa work?"

"A bakery/coffeehouse a few blocks from where she lives. She looks like an aging goth girl. Heavy dark makeup around the eyes. Spiky hairdo. Jet-black hair."

"You have her picture?"

"Found it on her Facebook page, so she might have deliberately chosen a weird snapshot."

"I'll look her up."

"But don't get any crazy ideas about questioning her, Sean. Anything I tell you is strictly to help you figure out how to keep Eve Worthington and her son away from Orson Bastion. You do not want to go up against him. He'll make those wild horses you're so fond of seem like puppy dogs."

"Gotcha."

"If I find out anything else, I'll let you know. In the meantime, no heroics. Death will not become you."

"No heroics," Sean promised. Unless Orson Bastion left him no other choice.

But neither would he sit around and do nothing until Eve gave in to Detective Reagan Conner's pressure and became bait for a madman.

ALYSSA WOKE WITH A splitting headache. Orson had always given her headaches, though in the old days they were usually caused by his slamming a fist into the side of her skull or shoving her into the wall.

She'd tell her mother when she got home from work, but it had never helped. Orson would deny everything and Lydia would believe his lies. As far as Alyssa's mother was concerned, Orson could do no wrong.

"Well, he's doing wrong now, Mom. He's killing innocent people and he's dragging me into his sordid games of revenge. And he's using your only grandson to blackmail me into doing his dirty work."

Alyssa picked up the silver frame that held the picture of her and her mother and threw it against the wall. The glass cracked and shards went flying about the room like cutting rain.

Lydia had helped make Orson into the monster he'd become. She'd let him get by with anything. Given him anything he'd wanted, even money for illegal drugs. He'd been her prince. Alyssa had been the miserable pauper, starved for even a smidgen of her mother's attention.

Alyssa didn't care anymore. All she cared about was Nick. He was a good kid. Not like Orson.

The piercing ring of the cell phone Orson had furtively supplied her with sent her head into orbit. She cradled her head with her right hand as she took the call.

"Did you get the money?"

"I tried, but no one will lend me that much," she replied. "I got behind on all my credit card bills when I was out of work. My credit score bottomed out. I told you that."

"I'm parked in front of Nick's school, Alyssa. I think it's time he meet his uncle."

"No. Leave him alone, Orson. Please, leave him be. I've got half the money. I'll give you that and get the rest tomorrow. Please don't touch Nick."

"I never said I'd hurt him. I'll just take him with me when I leave the country. Teach him to be a man. Just because you're my favorite sister."

His taunting laughter made her stomach roll.

"I'll have the money."

She had one last option—Frank—a loan shark who charged abominable rates of interest and would end up with her car and half of every paycheck. She'd be lucky if he left her with enough money to buy groceries. They'd likely be forced to live on the streets. And even at that, there was no guarantee that Frank would lend her that much.

She should have killed Orson herself, years ago, while he slept. The world would have been a better place.

Chapter Ten

Eve pulled her jeans jacket tight, glad she'd grabbed it when Sean had suggested a quick walk while Joey helped Collette feed the horses. The wind was howling this morning, the wind-chill factor making it seem colder than the forty-plus degrees the outside thermometer read.

She'd known from the insistence in his voice and the intensity in his eyes that this wouldn't be a pleasure walk. She'd been right, though she hadn't expected the topic of their conversation.

Eve slowed her pace. "I never heard that Orson's mother had committed suicide," she admitted, "but I can see how that, coupled with the failed parole attempt, might induce rage in a man like Orson."

"Rage that led to his attacking you three weeks after his mother's death."

"So you'd already considered the correlation between the incidents?"

"Yeah. It makes sense in a sick sort of way," Sean said, "especially if he was close to his mother."

"He talked about her during the therapy sessions," Eve admitted. "I got the sense that she was an enabler who contributed to his failure to accept responsibility for his actions."

"I thought psychopaths were born," Sean said, "and Orson sounds like a psychopath to me."

"The nature-versus-nurture argument is unimportant now, where Orson is concerned, but I'm not certain he's a true psychopath. He was twenty-eight when I found any evidence that he'd first been in trouble with the law, and that was when he murdered his stepbrother. Usually, psychopaths start showing signs of poor behavior control that get them in trouble with authority figures much earlier in life."

"Brand him what you want. The most important thing for me is keeping him away from you and Joey." Sean stopped walking when they reached the woodshed. He took Eve's hand and tugged her to a spot where the dilapidated structure blocked the worst of the wind.

His touch tangled with her emotions—heat against ice, desire against frustration.

"I know I came on strong last night, Eve, but you going back to Dallas with Orson still on the loose is too big a risk. There is no reason for you to leave the ranch. You're safe here."

"But for how long?" She leaned against the rough wood and propped one foot on the wall behind her. "Everyone predicted Orson would be back in prison by now. He's not. If he's really after me as Detective Conner said, then he'll find me. One way or another, he'll track me down unless he's stopped first."

"You said yourself that he'd never think to look here. And if he does, you have me, Troy and Dylan to protect you."

"With Orson, that might not be enough."

He brushed a windblown lock of hair from her face. His fingers lingered on her earlobe and his nearness consumed her. She tilted her head and met his gaze. His eyes were compelling, liquid depths she could drown in.

Unless her intuitive abilities had completely deserted her, the same urges that were buzzing through her were affecting him, too. He dropped his hand from her face and looked away.

"There's more, isn't there?" she asked.

"A little, but probably not important."

"What else did Wyatt tell you?"

"Orson has a sister living in San Antonio."

"Really? I had the impression he was an only child."

Eve listened to the facts about Alyssa Coleman. The decision was made even before Sean finished the explanation.

"I'm going to San Antonio and talk to Alyssa," she said.

"No way." Sean's muscles bunched, making his virile protectiveness even more pronounced.

"I have to talk to her," Eve insisted.

"What's the point? I'm sure the cops have already questioned her. Obviously, they didn't learn Orson's whereabouts from her, and there's no reason she'd tell you anything she didn't tell them."

"Maybe not intentionally, but if I can talk to her face-to-face, I may be able to figure out if Orson is still on his killing spree as Conner thinks, or if he's left the area or the country altogether."

"And you plan to just come out and ask her

these things? 'Hi, Alyssa. I hear your brother is out to kill me for blocking his parole. Want to get cozy and tell me how he's doing and where he's hiding out?'"

"She might want to tell me. For all I know, she could be just as afraid of him as I am. In any case, I need to talk to her. I won't even tell her who I am. It's not likely Orson carries my picture around in his wallet to show at family reunions."

"The cops may have a picture of you supplied by Detective Conner, and they'll be watching Alyssa's house just in case Orson is stupid enough to show up there."

"Then I'll visit her at work."

"There's no guarantee the cops aren't watching her there, as well."

"I'll go incognito."

"In what? Sunglasses and a hat?"

"Collette has a Mrs. Santa suit I can wear. The customers will think I work at a department store. Even Santa won't know me from the real thing."

"What about Joey?"

"I'm sure Collette will watch him for a few hours. He won't like my leaving him, but he's used to Collette and Troy, and even Dylan now. You saw how easily he left me to go feed the horses."

"I don't like it," Sean said.

"You can go with me or not, Sean. That's your choice. But I am going."

"I don't get it. Why take this risk when you don't have to, Eve? Why can't you just let me protect you?"

She linked her arm with his, craving his strength and needing him to understand.

"The longer Orson remains free, the greater the chance he'll find me. Even if you and Troy kill him before he hurts anyone, the violence will touch Joey. I can't let that happen—not if there's even the slightest chance I can do something to stop it."

Sean pulled her into his arms and held her so tight she could feel his heart beating against her chest. When he finally released her, he tangled his fingers in her hair at the nape of her neck.

"Okay, Mrs. Santa. Go get ready and I'll load the sleigh."

"Ho, ho, ho." But she wasn't laughing on the inside.

EVE REARRANGED HER short white wig, pulling the wiry strands of fake hair from beneath the fur collar. Visiting Alyssa Coleman might be a good idea, but this costume was not.

"How much farther?" she asked when they entered San Antonio.

"It should be right in this area."

"What's the name of the shop?"

"If Wyatt mentioned the name this morning, I missed it, but we're near her house, so we have to be near the shop."

"That could be it," Eve said, pointing to a green awning on the right side of the street.

Sean slowed and pulled to the curb. A sign on the walk outside the door announced that eggnog lattes and gingerbread coffees were the specialties of the day.

"You'll fit right in, Mrs. Santa, though with that pot belly, I'd lay off the calories."

"Not funny." She checked her reflection in the visor mirror one last time. "You have to admit I was right about being unrecognizable, though."

"I expect Dasher and Dancer to show up any minute."

"There are no reindeer in Texas."

She wrestled with the yards of red velvet while Sean held the door. A passing car honked. She looked up and waved cheerily.

She might as well get into the spirit of the costume.

Sean followed her up the short walk and through the door. They were met by delightful odors of coffee and treats baking in the oven. A display counter was filled with muffins, tarts, cookies, pies and layers of fresh gingerbread.

To Eve's surprise, the few patrons inside paid her and her costume little attention. Most were working at computers. A middle-aged woman was reading, and two young mothers were deep in conversation while their babies slept next to them in their infant seats.

To Eve's dismay, there was no sign of Alyssa, not if she still looked anything like the snapshot of her Sean had found on the computer. Even bypassing Austin traffic, it had taken them over two hours to get here, and it might all be for nothing.

A perky blonde stepped to the counter. "What can I get for you?"

"Just black coffee for me," Sean said.

She smiled and leaned over the counter provocatively, providing a glance of her assets. Eve wasn't surprised. A female of any age would have to be blind not to notice and get turned on by Sean.

"Is the coffee for here or to go?" the blonde asked.

"For here."

"In that case, have a seat anywhere and a waitress will be right with you to take your order."

Eve chose a table toward the back, so that the overhang from her bulky skirt wouldn't trip passing customers. A couple of minutes later, an equally vivacious and friendly waitress showed up at their table. Eve ordered a caramel latte, iced. She was perspiring under the costume.

"Is that all?" the waitress asked after she'd taken their orders. "The blueberry muffins are fresh out of the oven."

"Sure smell good," Sean said, "but I'll pass. Is Alyssa working today?"

"She's in the back, on break. Do you want me to get her for you?"

"If you don't mind."

"No problem."

Eve leaned toward him as the waitress hurried away. "That was smooth."

"You wanted to talk to Alyssa. I'm just trying to help."

She had wanted to see her. She still did—

only, now that they were here, she had no idea how to handle the confrontation.

Alyssa joined them and surprisingly slid into a chair next to Sean as if she were expecting him. Her expression was strained and the dark circles beneath her eyes made her look as if she hadn't slept for days.

She spread her hands on the table. "Did Frank send you?" she whispered.

Sean nodded.

If he was Frank, Eve wasn't the only one going incognito.

"Did you bring the money?"

He nodded again.

Eve had no idea what was going on.

"All five thousand dollars of it?"

"Just like you asked for."

Alyssa scanned the shop nervously. "We can't make the exchange here in the open."

"We can go to my truck. It's parked in front."

She shook her head. "I'll go to the ladies' room. Follow me in there and we'll make the exchange. Don't worry. Once you step through the arch, no will see which door you go in. And it locks."

Sean hesitated and Eve finally realized what was going down. Alyssa had mistaken Sean for someone else and he was playing along, hoping to get information about Orson.

"Not so quick," Eve said, keeping her voice low. "Before any money changes hands, we have to know where Orson is hiding out."

Alyssa's face turned ghostly white. "That wasn't part of the deal."

"It is now," Sean said.

"I don't know where he is. He'd never tell me that. I've agreed to all your demands. But I have to have that money." She started to shake, then looked to see if anyone was watching. "Please. I'll do anything you say, but I must have that money."

The woman was scared to death. Eve was certain that Orson was behind that fear. "I have the money with me," she said. "I'll follow you to the bathroom."

Alyssa walked away and Sean grabbed Eve's wrist. "What are you doing? I'm not sure what this is about, but we've pushed it as far as we can."

Eve stood, her skirt bouncing about like a red parachute until it knocked over a chair. This time people did turn to look. Eve took that opportunity to break loose from Sean.

"I'm giving her the money. Pay our tab and I'll meet you in the truck."

"You've lost your mind."

"Probably."

Sean caught up to her before she reached the bathroom door. "Crashing the ladies' restroom is a first for me, but Alyssa is the sister of a madman. You are not going anywhere with her without me."

Eve stepped inside, took the money from her oversize handbag and counted out fifty one-hundred-dollar bills while Sean watched. It was all the money she'd taken with her when she left Dallas, but she couldn't think of any better way to spend it.

"Take care," Eve whispered to Alyssa as she walked out of the ladies' room. "And stay safe."

She and Sean hurried through the shop and out the door.

He put a hand to the small of her back. "You just handed a woman you don't know five thousand dollars for, oh, let's see—zero information."

"And the money will go straight to Orson. And when it does, hopefully a cop will be there to make the arrest. I've given Detective Conner the bait he wants. All he has to do is trail Alyssa, and when she hands Orson the money, the cops nab him."

"That was fast thinking on your part," Sean admitted.

"About as fast as you becoming Frank. Now, how about getting Wyatt on the phone so he can put me in touch with Detective Conner?"

"Who knew Mrs. Santa was a detective at heart?"

"Who did you think squeals to Santa when you've been naughty or nice?

ONCE EVE HAD FINISHED her conversation with Detective Conner, she yanked off the wig and the hat and tossed them into the backseat. "The detective didn't sound all that appreciative," she said as she began wiggling out of the suffocating costume.

Sean cursed the traffic that forced him to keep his eyes and attention on the highway. "What did he say?"

"That I should not have gone to see Alyssa and that I was interfering with police business. Then he thanked me for calling."

In seconds, Eve had stripped down to pair of black slacks and a white T-shirt. Sean stole a look. Even in that she looked sexy, especially with the tips of her bare nipples outlined beneath the thin fabric.

"What did the detective say when you told him you expected to get your money back?"

"That he couldn't guarantee anything. Bottom line, he still thinks the surest way to apprehend Orson is for me to return to Dallas."

"An invitation that you surely turned down."

"That's when I told him that I thought I'd done my part. The rest was up to him."

Sean reached across the back of the seat and ruffled her hat hair. "You're pretty amazing."

"I thought you'd never notice."

"Seriously, you've held together great through all this. I can see now why Troy thinks so highly of you."

"He's your father, Sean. Would it be that difficult to just call him 'Dad'?"

"More difficult than you can imagine."

Sean plunged into his own thoughts while Eve put through a call to Collette to check on Joey. Eve was a great mother.

Like his mother had been. He had trouble remembering her face these days. Instead, the images were confused with the dozens of pictures of her his grandparents had kept on display.

What Sean remembered about her were moments, prisms of love captured in time. Her hair falling about his face when she kissed him good-night. Her voice when she sang along with the radio. How she'd stay up with him when he was sick and read him stories.

How she'd cried with him when Sinbad had gotten sick and they'd thought he might have to be put down. Mom had been love.

Troy had been his hero, a man's man, the guy Sean had always looked up to. Making his father proud of him had been the greatest feeling in the world.

And then it had all come crumbling down into a pile of ash that still poisoned his mind. So, yes—it was impossible to look at the man and call him "Dad."

And dwelling on this would get him nowhere.

"How's Joey?" he asked, once Collette was off the phone.

"Collette says he keeps asking when we'll be home, but I talked to him, and he seems fine. A little anxious, but fine."

"Then what do you say to stopping for a quick bite? It's two hours past my lunch time."

"I could eat," she said. "But I'm not dressed

for the occasion, and I'm definitely not putting that velvet monstrosity back on."

"Not likely anyone would recognize either one of us, now that we're nowhere near Alyssa Coleman, but I was thinking we'd just find a fast-food drive-through. There are several listed for the next exit, and there's a rest stop a couple of miles down the freeway. We can just pull off the road and eat there."

"I could go for a burger and fries."

Sean pulled into the exit lane. Ten minutes later they were parked beneath a couple of spreading oaks. He lowered the windows and breathed in a huge gulp of fresh air. The wind had died down since morning, and there wasn't a cloud in the sky. It was a perfect hill country December day.

Except that Eve still had a dangerous escaped convict who wanted her dead. If she hadn't, she wouldn't need his protection. He'd never have met her. He wouldn't be sitting here now, thinking how much he'd like to kiss her until the hunger inside him melted away.

"Why did you come back to Mustang Run, Sean?"

"I'd quit my job. Dylan had been after me to visit the ranch, so I started driving in this direction. The next thing I knew, I was here and you were coming at me with a knife."

And the desire she'd awakened in him that night was about to push him over the edge of reason now.

"Did you live with your grandparents after your mother died?"

"I lived with my uncle Bill. He was a confirmed old bachelor who taught high school history. He didn't talk much, read too much and hated Troy for killing his baby sister."

"Was he good to you?"

"He wasn't mean. I felt alone a lot. But he paid for me to have horseback riding lessons, and as soon as I was old enough, I started working at a riding stable near our house. I spent as much time there as possible. That might have something to do with my interacting better with horses than with people."

"You do just fine with some people," Eve assured him, "especially with Joey."

"He's a good kid."

"I know, but I can't help but worry about him. He never talks about his father's death anymore, and he's gotten much better. But I hate to even imagine what it would do to him to face that kind of violence again."

"I didn't realize his father had died a violent death."

"Brock was killed in a freakish drive-by shooting two years ago. We'd never had anything like that in our neighborhood before, and we haven't had one since. The police decided it was random, or possibly a case of mistaken identity."

Eve wrapped her arms around her chest, shrinking inside herself. He ached to hold her, but the timing didn't seem right.

"That must have been incredibly hard on you and Joey."

She nodded her head. "Joey was with him. Miraculously, he wasn't hit."

"He saw his father killed?"

"At close range. Blood from the gunshot wound dripped all over his shoes."

Poor kid." But it explained why Joey clung so to his mother and why he was shy and fearful around strangers. And why she was so fiercely protective of him. Sean had needed reassurance like that when *his* mother died and he'd been much older than Joey.

"You must miss Brock very much," he said. It wasn't a question.

"I hate that Brock was killed and that Joey lost his father, but the sad truth is that Brock and I were getting a divorce. He was leaving me for an aerobics instructor at the gym where he worked out."

The man had to be crazy to even think of leaving Eve.

"A philandering husband murdered in a quiet, upscale neighborhood," Eve continued. "As you can imagine, it caused quite a stir. For a few days, I think I was even considered a suspect in the murder, so I know how devastating that can be."

Eve shifted to face Sean. "It must have been a million times worse for your father. He was convicted of killing a woman he worshipped."

If *Troy was innocent,* Sean thought.

"I left my position with the prison system after Brock was killed, so that I could be with Joey full-time. He needed me at home, and I'd already decided to find a new job. I didn't think I'd ever feel comfortable again at the Huntsville facility, after Orson's attack."

The facts bucked around in Sean's mind. "How long was it before the attack that your husband was killed?"

"Two weeks to the day."

"And no one ever questioned whether or not Orson was behind Brock's murder?"

"Orson was in prison. There was no way he could have killed him."

"That doesn't eliminate the possibility that he had someone else do it for him, perhaps someone he'd met in prison."

Eve wadded her napkin, crushing it in her hands. "If that's true, then even back then Orson had just methodically and determinedly set out to destroy me."

Sean could not let that happen. And he simply couldn't fight his need for her another second.

He leaned across the seat, tugged her towards him and kissed her. Her lips parted as she kissed him back, over and over, until passion swallowed up everything but the two of them and the animal-like need roaring inside him.

But then Eve pulled away, and he felt bereft.

"We should get back to the ranch," she murmured.

"Right." He could make it that long, but how would he ever make it through the night without pillaging those sweet lips again?

He'd never wanted a woman more. And that frightened him.

SEAN SLOWED, AND A WAVE OF adrenaline shot through him as he spotted the strange car in the driveway in front of the ranch house. Troy was standing on the front porch next to an attractive woman who looked to be about his age, only much better preserved.

"Looks like Troy has company," Eve said. "I never considered that when I asked him and Collette to watch Joey. I guess I should have."

Sean didn't bother hiding his anger. "He knows how important it is that no one knows you're here."

"Maybe he didn't know she was coming."

Sean's irritation wasn't appeased, though he realized the sick rolling inside him wasn't just about Troy's lack of consideration for Eve.

This was his mother's house. The porch where Troy had sat with her on warm summer nights. Sean's mother, that Eve had claimed Troy worshipped.

He'd been out of prison mere months. It sure hadn't taken him long to find a replacement.

The woman was vaguely familiar, but Sean couldn't place her. She met him at the steps, all smiles as if she couldn't wait to see him.

"Sean Ledger. It's about time you came

back to the ranch. I bet you don't even remember me."

"Can't say that I do."

"Ruthanne Foley. I was your mother's best friend."

And suddenly Sean remembered exactly who she was.

Chapter Eleven

Ruthanne had been in and out of their house all the time when Sean was a kid. Her husband had come over a lot, too. Sean hadn't liked him. He talked loud and was always telling Sean and his brothers they should go outside and play, like it was his house instead of theirs.

He'd liked Ruthanne until the night he saw her with his dad out at the horse barn when neither of them knew Sean was watching. She'd tried to kiss his dad, but then his dad had seen Sean and pushed her away.

Sean had never told anyone what he saw that night, not even his brothers. But he'd hated it when Ruthanne came around after that.

For all Sean knew, it could have been as innocent on Troy's part as when Sasha

Cahill had tried to jump his bones, but the old resentment rattled him all the same.

"Ruthanne heard I was sick and dropped by to bring a casserole dish," Troy said. "She's just leaving."

"News travels fast," Sean said.

"I ran into a nurse friend who works the E.R.," Ruthanne said. "She told me the ambulance had bought Troy in with a heart attack the other night. I tried to call him, but he never answers the phone."

"Doctor's orders," Troy quipped. "I need my rest."

Troy was still holding the casserole dish, so, evidently, he'd met Ruthanne on the porch and not invited her inside. If they'd arrived a few minutes later, he and Eve could have avoided her altogether.

Ruthanne smoothed the front of her snugly fitted sweater and turned to Eve. "You must be a friend of Sean's."

"She is," Troy lied. "This is Ellen. She lives in Houston."

A nice recovery, Sean had to admit. Having anyone see Eve at the ranch was worrisome. He and Eve followed their hellos with a quick goodbye and left Troy and Ruthanne standing on the porch. They closed the door firmly behind them and Eve went off in search of Joey and Collette.

He followed to make sure she found them. When she joined them in the protected garden where Collette was on her knees helping Joey build a stone bridge for his cars, he returned to the kitchen. Troy was standing at the kitchen counter, closing the top on a bottle of pills. Troy swallowed a white tablet and chased it with a glass of water.

"I'm sorry Ruthanne ran into Eve like that, but I had nothing to do with her coming over. She just showed up. But no harm was done. She has no idea who Eve is."

"Did she see Joey?"

"No. Collette took him to the back of the house when we saw the car drive up."

Sean wanted to say more, but it was his own frustration pushing him. Troy couldn't have very well just run off Ruthanne with a rifle.

Sean went to the counter for a cup of coffee.

"I'm limited to a cup a day," Troy said, "but Collette made a fresh pot after lunch. It should still be drinkable."

Sean took a sip. "It's fine."

"How did the meeting with Bastion's sister go?"

"It netted her a gain of five thousand dollars."

Sean filled him in on the details and even mentioned the possibility that Orson might have had Brock Worthington killed.

Troy scratched his chin. "You're right. That sounds just like something he'd do. I can't believe I didn't think of that."

"We don't have proof," Sean said, "but the timing sure makes it appear suspicious." He carried his coffee to the table. The entire top was covered in computer printouts, yellowed newspaper and scribbled notes.

He found a spot just big enough for his cup. "What's this?"

Troy joined him at the table. "I've been collecting information on crimes committed in Mustang Run and neighboring towns within a year either way of the time your mother was murdered."

It was quite an impressive collection. "Did you gather all this by yourself?"

"Most of it, but Abel Drake's put me on some leads. He has a friend who was a Ranger back then, Trent Fontaine. Trent came up with some information I would have never found."

"Like what?"

"An alleged rape in the northern part of the county one month before your mother was shot and killed. The woman claimed she came home and found a man inside her house rifling through her cabinets. He raped her, but left out the back door when her husband drove up. She called the authorities but was too embarrassed to press charges, so there was never any formal record of the crime."

"Were there others like that?"

"A rape and murder in a neighboring county that was never solved."

"What about forensic evidence?"

"Apparently there was nothing that could identify the killer. But back then CSI teams weren't what they are now, especially in rural areas. No one ever checked fibers or hairs or any of the other evidence they rely so heavily on now."

Sean scanned a couple of the newspaper articles. "You've done some pretty thorough digging. Who did you say hooked you up with the ranger?"

"Abel Drake. He's an old friend, used to live in these parts, but he has a ranch just east of Dallas now."

Sean spent the next hour going over the information spread across the table. The work represented a lot of time and effort. It was the kind of thing you'd expect from a man who was actually looking for his wife's killer.

OTHER THAN AT DINNER, Sean had seen little of Eve since they returned from San Antonio. She'd spent most of her time with Joey, who'd at least temporarily reverted to clinging and dogging her every step.

Sean understood Joey's deep-rooted anxiety better since he'd heard that the boy was there when his dad had died. He'd seen the blood up close and personal, the way Sean had when his mother had been murdered. Joey had been younger, likely understood less, but Joey's father had been alive and walking down the street with him one minute and dead the next.

There was too much violence in this country, too many kids who lived with nightmarish images forever seared into their minds.

Sean had buried much of his pain and fear deep inside him. Oddly, he became better at dealing with his own issues when he began to work with horses full-time. Horses responded to body language rather than words, to experiences instead of lectures. They made slow but steady progress, as long as the environment was conducive, trust was there and their basic needs were met.

Seems it was the same for people, even kids. It was pretty basic when you thought about it.

Except when you were dealing with men like Orson Bastion. Men without conscience or guilt, who killed without remorse whenever it suited them.

And Sean had no doubt that the kind of evil Orson possessed had started early in his life. Just because they had no record of it didn't mean it hadn't occurred.

Troy Ledger was not an evil man. So, if he had killed Sean's mother all those years ago, it would have taken some incredibly strong motivation or temporary insanity. But Troy hadn't claimed temporary insanity. He'd claimed innocence. And now he was, at the very least, going through the motions of looking for his wife's killer.

Sean's hodgepodge of thoughts collided with his equally jumbled emotions. The quietness of the house only added to the mix. His father had retired for the night. Eve was still back in her bedroom, though it was well past Joey's bedtime.

He was starting to think Eve was merely

avoiding him. She'd thrown herself whole-heartedly into this afternoon's kiss. He was pretty sure it had left her reeling the way it had him. But she'd had time to think about it since then. She might just be smart enough to figure out that adding fiery passion to a deadly situation wasn't all that smart.

"Sean."

He turned at the sound of Eve's voice, though he'd been so lost in his thoughts he hadn't heard her approach. She was standing in the doorway, wearing the pale blue robe that always fired his imagination about the body beneath it. Desire rocked through him and his body hardened into a painful, throbbing need that devoured his control.

He walked over, took one end of the dangling belt between his fingers and tugged. The robe fell open revealing nothing but naked flesh.

Eve slipped her arms around his neck. "I got tired of waiting for you to come to bed."

Chapter Twelve

Sean's blood ran fire-hot through his veins as he picked up Eve and carried her to his room. Her arms and legs wrapped around him. Her fingers curled in his hair. But it was her kisses that drove him wild. Deep, wet, greedy, as if she couldn't get enough of him.

He let her slide down his body until her feet touched the floor. The pressure against his hard need triggered a thousand new emotions, all of them wild and tempestuous. He throbbed with a need so earthy and unfettered that he could barely turn the lock on the door.

Once he did, it was déjà vu, a repeat of night one. A sensual, frantic tangle of legs, arms and bodies. Only, this time Eve was the aggressor and there was no knife. No hesitation. No restraint.

She backed him against the wall, ripped

open his shirt and smothered his bare chest with kisses. He tugged the robe from her shoulders and let it puddle at their feet. Kicking it out of the way, he fit his hands beneath her firm little buttocks, lifting and fitting her against him.

She pulled away just enough to slide her hands between them and unsnap his jeans. Lowering the zipper with one frantic jerk, she traced a searing trail down the length of his erection with her fingertips.

He should slow down, but he couldn't, especially not now, not with Eve's hands and mouth exploring him and finding every spot that drove him mad.

He slid his hands between her legs. She was already slick with desire. Blood rushed to his head. He'd never been this hot for a woman, never been this dizzy with desire. Never been so damned out of control.

He wrapped his hands around his need, trying desperately to hold back. "I have protection in my wallet."

"I haven't been with another man in years," she said. "After Brock, I got a clean bill of health. And there's no chance of pregnancy this week."

"It's been sixteen months for me. Two clean checkups since then."

Sean exhaled in relief and then was hit again by passion so intense he could barely stand. He lifted Eve and fit her over the throbbing length of his organ. She moaned as he thrust inside her.

And then there was no holding back. They exploded together in a frenzy of release that seemed to rock the whole room.

"I should have—"

Eve silenced him with a finger against his lips. "No shoulda-wouldas. That was exactly what I needed. The only question is how long before we can do it again."

If she kept curling around him as she was doing now, the wait would be incredibly short. This time, when he picked her up he carried her to his bed.

EVE CUDDLED IN SEAN'S ARMS, feeling as if she'd been painted inside and out with a sweet, golden brush of pleasure. The past week had been a nightmare. Tonight's sensual frenzy had provided the perfect release for the multitude of emotions that had run roughshod over her ever since she left Dallas for Willow Creek Ranch.

But it wasn't only about release for her. It was about Sean and the way he excited her by just brushing her shoulder when they passed in the hallway. About his blatant virility and the way he wore his jeans. About the way he handled Joey and looked after both of them.

She trailed her fingers down his abs. "Are you sleepy?"

"No, just regrouping."

"Tell me about you."

"There's nothing to tell. What you see is what you get."

"I know you've been in relationships. What happened that kept them from leading to marriage?"

"Nothing traumatic. I was engaged in college. We were planning to get married after we graduated and both got jobs."

"That seems smart."

"Real smart. It gave us time to figure out that we were heading in different directions. I couldn't see myself in a life that didn't involve horses. Once she got a job with a Madison Avenue advertising firm, she didn't see herself living anywhere but New York."

"So she called off the marriage?"

"It was a mutual parting of the ways."

"Were there others? I mean, others you were serious about? I'm not asking for stats."

"Good. I never kiss and tell—unless the kisses are as memorable as yours." He smiled at her. "Right now I'm thinking I should probably call everyone I know and shout about the thrill of you."

He kissed her again to make his point. Kissing made it really difficult to think coherently. But she did want to know why he was still single when he would have made such a marvelous husband and father.

"I'm being serious," she said.

"So was I." He stretched and put his hands behind his head, as if he needed to separate a bit from her before he could focus on the past. "I almost made it to the altar three years ago."

"What happened that time?"

"That time it was all my fault. Angie was great. We were the same age, both twenty-eight. And we both loved horses. She managed the dude ranch her father owned up in Colorado. I was working for a privately run horse-abuse facility at the time. I figured it was time I settled down, and this time all the external factors were in my favor."

"Only, you never married."

"Nope. A week before the wedding, I realized I couldn't go through with it. Something was missing. I had no idea what. I decided then that I was not meant for long-term relationships. So I paid all the nonrefundable wedding expenses, quit my job and moved on."

"What happened to Angie?"

"She was furious with me—until she met her real Mr. Right. Then she called and thanked me. I went to their wedding. They have twin girls now."

At least Eve knew where she stood with Sean. He was not available for a long-term relationship. *So don't go building a dream around him,* she warned herself. She could get her head around that. It wasn't as if she was already planning to pick out furniture with him.

But as for not falling for him, it was way too late to convince her heart of that.

Sean turned and pulled her close again, nuzzling his face in her cleavage. "Time to make up for shortchanging you."

"You didn't. I asked—" She stopped talking as he slid his hand between her legs and sent vibrations of anticipation dancing through every inch of her. He clearly wasn't referring to their conversation.

"So show me the best you have to offer," she teased, easily falling back into the pleasure zone.

The lovemaking started all over again, this time slower, but no less exciting. Sean cupped her breasts, licking and sucking the nipples until they tingled, creating sensations in them she'd never imagined possible.

Impulsively she arched toward him.

"I love the way you open up to me, Eve. Sensually. Uninhibited. Like a woman who knows what she wants."

"What I want is you, Sean."

He kissed his way to her navel, teasing it with his tongue while his fingers explored her most intimate niches. She opened her legs wide, crazy for every touch, giddy from the surges of desire that sprung from deep in her core.

The sweet ache between her thighs intensified. He moved until his rock-hard erection throbbed against them.

"I want you inside me, Sean. Deep inside me."

"Once I'm there, I won't be able to hold off long."

"Then we'll explode together."

She was hot and slick and so ready for him that the first thrust almost sent her into orbit. Making love with Sean might not be this earth-shattering every time, but she couldn't imagine that she'd ever not want him inside her.

His breath came in hard, quick spurts. She closed her eyes and let the thrill take her, riding with him, to the crest and beyond.

Time stopped for an instant and then started again as Sean's spent body rolled off hers. He slid onto his back and pulled her into his arms.

"You're something else," he whispered.

"Is that good?"

"Nope. It's perfection."

The perfection was the two of them together. And even temporary perfection beat mediocrity hands down.

EVE SLEPT UNTIL SHE FELT A tug on her sheet.

"It's morning, Momma. I gotta go feed the horses."

Eve rubbed the dregs of sleep from her eyes, thankful she'd sneaked back to the room she shared with Joey and put on her pajamas in the wee hours of the morning. Eve glanced at the bedside clock and then back at her son.

It was indeed morning, ten before eight. Joey was already dressed in jeans, a blue pullover that was inside out and his boots.

She swung her legs over the side of the bed, biting back a groan at the unexpected ache in her thighs.

"Why don't you go visit with Troy while I get dressed," she suggested.

"I better go wake up Sean first. He's taking me horseback riding."

"What makes you think that?"

"He told me."

"When?"

"Yesterday, when me and him had a glass of chocolate milk on the back steps. You were in the bathroom."

That was the first she'd heard about it, but it made sense. Her leaving Joey with Collette yesterday had revived Joey's separation fears. The only time Joey had let her out of his sight after she returned from San Antonio was when she was in the shower. Leave it to Sean to give him something to look forward to.

"If Sean said he'd take you for a ride, I'm

sure he will. But don't wake him. He'll come find you when he's ready."

"Okay." Joey picked up his hat and carried it with him. He wouldn't want to waste time coming back for it when Collette showed up to get him for the feeding chore.

Eve owed Gordon Epps a big thank-you for suggesting she and Joey hide out at Willow Creek Ranch. Had she stayed in Dallas... The possible outcomes were too distressing to consider.

She rinsed her face with cold water in the bathroom and then hurried to dress, choosing jeans and a long-sleeved, turquoise shirt that was one of her favorites. Using the mirror in her compact to check the results, she brushed on a hint of blush and smear of lip gloss.

Once she brushed and smoothed her hair, she looked closely in the mirror, amazed that last night's lovemaking didn't make her face light up like neon. But if there was any visible sign at all, it was in her eyes.

Now all she needed was word that Orson Bastion had been captured. Her hand was on the doorknob, when the now-familiar cold draft of air swirled around her, as if the ghost of Helene Ledger was trying to warn her of something.

The coolness vanished and the room became almost suffocating in contrast. Apprehension prickled the flesh on the back of Eve's neck. Rationality returned slowly. When it did, Eve dismissed all thoughts of ghosts and put in a call to Gordon Epps.

She was about to leave a message when he picked up the call. "Hello."

"Hi, Gordon. Hope I didn't disturb you."

"I was on the other line with Detective Conner."

She took a deep breath and dropped to the edge of the bed. "Bad news?"

"No news, except that he thinks you should return to Dallas. And it's obvious that he believes I'm in frequent contact with you. He pressured me again for a way to reach you."

"I hate that I'm forcing you to lie."

"I kind of got myself into that by calling you originally. But I think maybe you should listen to Conner, Eve."

"You think I should return to Dallas."

"Troy's a good guy and a tough old buzzard, but he's sick. It's unlikely either Dylan or Sean have experience with men like Orson. Besides, I think it might take a whole police department to stop Orson Bastion. Conner sounds as if he's ready to supply that now."

"If I agree to be bait."

"It's just my opinion, Eve. You do what you think is best, but don't ever start taking your safety for granted. You can't when you're dealing with Orson."

"I know that."

But she'd already given them bait. All they had to do was follow the money. She decided not to mention that to Gordon. She'd already involved him too deeply in her problems.

"I'll give it some thought," she said.

They finished the conversation, and this time when she started to the kitchen there were no cold drafts. Optimism filtered though the anxiety. With any luck, Orson would go to Alyssa for the money today and be back in prison before dark.

If not, she'd have to reconsider Gordon's advice. If it came down to her having to face Orson, then Conner and the Dallas Police Department really were her best option for getting out alive.

"Now, we're talking serious psychopath."

"None of this is etched in stone," Wyatt reminded Sean. "It's not even allegations at this point, but just findings I thought you might find interesting."

Sean found them interesting, all right. Eve would find them bone-chilling. It was just one more thing he'd have to hit her with. But it shed even more light on the criminal mind of Orson Bastion.

"What's the likelihood any of this will be followed up on?" Sean asked.

"The first drowning falls under my jurisdiction."

"Does that mean you feel a cold case being opened?"

"At least a preliminary investigation. We'll decide whether or not to move forward after that. A reopening of Brock Worthington's murder trial would fall into the hands of the Dallas Police Department, unless there's an excuse to bring the FBI in on it."

Sean's suspicions about Bastion being involved in Brock's murder had led to Sean calling Wyatt this morning. The new information Wyatt had gathered had been lagniappe. If possible, the influx of data raised the danger bar even more.

He looked out the window and saw Eve and Joey returning from the horse barn. Joey was skipping along beside her, his boots kicking up dust. Sunlight shimmered in Eve's hair. She was smiling.

He didn't have the heart to chill her bones just yet.

"Gotta go," Sean said.

"Yeah, me too," Wyatt answered. "It's hectic on the homicide front this morning."

"Thanks for keeping me posted and for letting me bounce ideas off of you."

"No problem. Just watch your step and keep a cool head on your shoulders. Duking it out with a psycho is never a fair fight."

Eve and Jocy stepped through the back door, lighting up the room as he broke the connection. A new plan was rapidly forming in Sean's mind.

Joey raced over to Sean. "Can we go horseback riding now?"

"I don't see why not, as long as your mother okays it."

"Can't my momma go, too?"

"Wouldn't be the same without her."

"Will you go, Momma?" Joey pleaded.

"Sure. Someone has to look after you hombres."

Troy joined them in the kitchen, no doubt lured by Joey's excited voice. "Did I hear someone say horseback riding?"

"Yes," Joey said. "Do you wanna go with us? You can ride your own horse."

"I'd love to, but I'm afraid it would go against doctor's orders. But I've been thinking. Do you know what this house needs?"

"I bet I know," Joey said. "It needs a dog."

Eve put a hand on Joey's shoulders. "Why do you think we need a dog?"

"When I wanted one for my birthday, you said our yard was too small and that we didn't have a fence. But his yard is bigger than a bunch of parks, and it has lots of fences."

"Good point," Troy said. "We do need a dog around here, but I was thinking we need a Christmas tree. After all, it is December."

Joey's eyes grew wide. "Can we go buy a tree?"

"No need to do that," Troy said. "Cedars grow like weeds around here. I noticed a patch of them on that knoll west of Dylan's house. Several that looked to be a perfect size for a tree. I thought maybe you guys could pick one while you're out riding. If you find one you like, you can go back later, chop it down and bring it home in the back of the truck. That way you won't mess up the branches, dragging it behind your mount."

"Not a bad idea," Sean said. In fact, getting a tree for Joey was an excellent idea. It just surprised Sean that it had come from Troy. Seventeen years in prison, but he still understood what a Christmas tree meant to a kid.

"If you call, I can drive out and meet you with an ax and the truck," Troy said. "As long as you call before two. Dylan's driving me to the doctor shortly after that."

"Are you okay?" Eve asked.

"I'm fine. This is just a routine checkup, so don't go making a fuss. You just find us a tree," Troy said. "Helene always liked one that was just an inch or so shy of the ceiling."

His voice caught on Sean's mother's name. And a ridiculous knot formed in Sean's throat. "We'll find a tree. Now let's get out of here," he said, before he got tangled up in the facts, suspicions and bittersweet memories that would drag him back into his own nightmarish past.

There was already too much talk of Christmas, old memories and new horrors about a killer who wanted Eve dead. And the day was only beginning.

EVE FELT AS IF SHE WERE living in an alternate universe as she watched Joey dash around the deep green cedars, choosing first one and then another as the perfect Christmas tree. He'd made more emotional strides in the last week than he'd made in the past two years. And this at a time when he'd been ripped from his home and plugged into a group of strangers.

The wide-open spaces seemed to work like a safety valve, giving Joey room to let off steam without constantly being inundated by different people coming and going, as he was at the crowded park near their Dallas home.

He was mesmerized by the horses, so much so that he'd bonded with Collette in order to help her feed them. That, and the fact that she offered no threat. She didn't bug him about being a baby when he wanted his mother around. She was loving and gentle and fun to be with.

Dylan and Troy were a different story. Joey was slightly wary around them, but if Troy kept coming up with ideas like Christmas trees, he'd move up the friendship ladder fast.

But Sean was the hero, the one to emulate. He had a way of making Joey feel independent without pushing.

Joey had stopped running around the trees now, and he and Sean were on their knees, studiously examining something in the grass.

Eve left her comfortable spot on the grassy knoll and went over to join them.

"What have you two found so fascinating?" she asked.

"I saw a spider," Joey said, "but it got away before I could show it to Sean."

"Good," Eve said. "I like spiders that run away."

"Aw, I wanted to catch him and see if he was poisonous."

"I have a better idea," she said. "Let's pretend he is and leave him alone."

Sean gave Joey a very light but manly punch on the arm. "Women. They just don't get bugs."

"Have you decided on a tree?" Eve asked.

"We're stuck between two choices," Sean said. "Shall we let your mother have the deciding vote, Joey?"

"I betcha she picks the skinny one."

Joey pointed out the trees. The choice was a no-brainer. "The fat one will take up half the family room," she said.

"I told you she'd pick the skinny one."

"The skinny one it is," Sean said. "Dylan and I will come for it later today."

Eve eyed the tree again. "I hope it's not too tall." But it wouldn't be her and Joey's

Christmas tree. Surely Orson would be captured by Christmas and they'd be back in Dallas. Away from the horses and wide-open spaces of the ranch.

Away from Sean. He was not a forever kind of guy.

Joey pointed to an aging oak tree about thirty yards away. It had apparently been hit by lightning at some time in the past, and one huge limb fell almost to the ground before stretching skyward again. "Can I go climb in that tree?"

"You might fall and—sure," she said, reconsidering. "Have fun, but be careful."

"A giant step for mothering," Sean said when Joey was out of earshot.

"I'm trying," she said. "It's hard to admit I got in the habit of being overly protective, especially with my being a psychiatrist."

Sean took her hand in his and pulled her down to the grass beside him. "I can see how protection can get to be a habit."

He toyed with a lock of her hair and for a second she thought he was going to kiss her. Instead, he let go of her hand and stared into space.

"Is something wrong?"

"I talked to Wyatt this morning while

you and Joey were helping Collette feed the horses."

"Not more bad news. If it is, I don't want to hear it. All I want to know about Orson is that he's been arrested."

"I don't have any news that changes the current situation for the better or worse," Sean assured her.

"Then what is it?"

"There have been two other unexplained deaths that could be connected to Bastion."

"You mean besides Brock's?"

"Right. The first death happened when Orson was just twelve years old and swimming with a friend in a backyard pool."

"Did the pool belong to Orson's family?"

"No, it belonged to a family that was out of town. They managed to break the lock on the gate to get in. Details are sketchy, since the drowning was quickly concluded to be an accident, but the other boy was said to be a good swimmer. Orson claimed he got his foot caught in the drain somehow and got trapped underwater. He said he tried to save his friend, but that he died before he could get him loose."

"That could have happened."

"It could have. What makes it suspect is

that Orson didn't admit to being with him when he drowned until another neighbor said he'd seen Orson break the lock on the gate. When confronted by the police, Orson admitted to being there, but said he got scared and ran home when the kid died in the water. The victim's body was found on top of the water with bruises around his legs."

Eve shivered at the thought of Orson's being capable of such cruelty when he was only six years older than Joey was right now. And if Orson had killed that boy, some family had needlessly suffered through the heartbreak of losing their child.

She looked to make certain Joey was still okay. He waved and grinned. She placed her hand on Sean's knee. "And the second instance?"

"It happened much later, during Orson's sophomore year in college. He and a girlfriend went to Cancún on spring break. She was found dead in the room, overdosed on booze and drugs."

"That one doesn't sound particularly suspicious."

"Except that the young woman's friends all said that she'd had a bad trip on acid the year before and that she hadn't touched illegal drugs since. It was also reported that Orson had flown into a jealous rage the day before and had accused her of getting it on with another reveler."

"But the death was still ruled an accident?"

"Yes. If Orson was involved in either of those deaths, he managed to present convincing arguments in his favor and was never considered a serious murder suspect."

"One of the characteristics of a true psychopath," Eve said. "Along with signs of cruelty showing up early in life. That's what was confusing in Orson's profile. Now even that part makes sense."

Sean put an arm around her shoulders. "Both events could be circumstance. I didn't tell you this to upset you, but I didn't want to keep things from you, either."

"I need to know the truth. It helps me to know exactly what I'm facing."

"You're facing a lunatic."

"That's not a psychological term."

"I'm not a psychological kind of guy. I'm more into the commonsense, big picture approach."

"Which means?"

"Sitting around waiting for Orson to either

get captured or make his next murderous move is hell on your nerves, and it's not that great on mine."

"I can leave."

"Yeah, wondering if you're about to be killed at any second would make me feel great."

She threw up her hands. "What do you want, Sean? I'm definitely open to suggestions."

"Let's get out of here. The three of us. We'll fly to Europe, take a winter vacation until Bastion is captured. It's not like I've got a job to hurry back to. And I've always wanted to visit Venice."

"It could take weeks or months before Orson is captured."

"It could take years, but we don't have to make a lifetime of decisions right now."

"You don't ever have to make a lifetime of decisions, Sean. You said as much last night."

"I knew that would come back to haunt me."

"I'm sorry," Eve said. "That just slipped out before I thought. I know you're trying to help, and I appreciate it."

"We can get a flight out tomorrow afternoon at three. They have first-class seats available and I have plenty of points to get them."

"How would a horse whisperer ever acquire that many points?"

"I'm good at what I do. A billionaire from Spain flew me over once a month for two years to work with his favorite mount."

"So you just checked the airline schedules without even asking me?"

Sean tucked a thumb under her chin and tilted it, forcing her to meet his gaze. "Say yes, Eve. I'll take care of everything else."

This was all happening so fast. On the surface, she loved the idea of running away to Italy with Sean. But if they stayed too long, she'd only fall harder for him. Joey would get used to having him in his life, only to lose him when this was over.

"I have to have time to think about it."

"I don't see what there is to think about. If nothing else, we'd have a great vacation."

He made it sound so easy. Maybe it was. "I'll give you an answer in the morning."

"And within twenty-four hours the three of us can be strolling along the Grand Canal."

ORSON KICKED THE BACK of the chair, sending the cheap piece of spindly wood banging against the wall of the deserted camp house where he'd been hanging out.

He hadn't broken out of prison to live like this. Mexico and señoritas by the dozens were waiting on him. He'd made three major mistakes in his life. The first was letting himself get arrested for the death of his worthless stepbrother.

The second was trusting his former cell-mate Bodie Greene to follow Orson's exact plans for the murder of Brock Worthington. If Bodie hadn't screwed up, Eve would have gotten life in prison for the deed and Orson wouldn't have had to go to all this trouble to kill her now.

The third mistake was in not killing Eve when he'd had his hands around her bony neck. One more squeeze and she'd have died gasping for breath. He couldn't even blame Troy Ledger for that. The guy was just doing what your average halfway moral jerk did— saving a damsel in distress.

Orson wasn't average. He was Mensa-smart and brazen enough to do what other bastards in the world were too dumb to do. This wasn't how he'd planned to spend his last night in Texas, but it would be good enough to send him off with a bang.

He laughed at his own clever turn of thought.

Tomorrow he'd get the money from Alyssa and then he'd pay a visit to the basketball court in the park near his nephew's school. It would be much easier to kidnap him from there. Nick would love Mexico oncc he got used to it. And Alyssa would send money for years, in hopes Orson would keep her son safe.

It was a win-win situation.

Not quite as perfect as he'd planned. But close enough. All he'd miss was seeing Eve Worthington's face when her world went up in smoke.

Chapter Thirteen

Sean watched as Eve slipped quietly from his room. He'd tried to coax her into staying longer, but she insisted she needed sleep if she was going to make a make a major decision in the morning. And if she stayed, they both knew that one restless turn and touch in the night and they'd be in the throes of passion again.

The lovemaking tonight had been every bit as hot, as consuming, as it had been the first time. In some ways, it was even better, though he wasn't sure that was possible. He was learning where to touch her and how much pressure to use to make her moan in pleasure. Eve seemed to instinctively know how to drive him mad with wanting her.

But when the lovemaking was over, he'd felt the tension developing between them like sharp edges on a sparkling diamond. He'd probably been too honest with her last night when he said he'd never been able to make a relationship work long-term. But they sure wouldn't have a chance of making this work if he started out lying to her.

Yet, here he was, lying to himself, pretending that he actually had a chance with her. She needed him now, but what was the chance she'd want him in her life when the crisis was over?

Too restless to think about sleep, Sean got out of bed and pulled on his jeans and the denim jacket he'd left thrown over the back of a chair. He'd never owned a robe in his life. Didn't plan to start now.

He wandered down the hallway to the extension that created one wall of the courtyard garden. He hadn't been in it since he returned. His mother had loved that spot, and Sean hadn't been ready to buck up against those memories.

He wasn't sure he was ready now, but he found his way there anyway. The garden was secluded, entered on one side through a guest room and on the other side via the master suite. Needless to say, Sean did not go though the room where his father slept in the big iron bed he'd once shared with Sean's mother.

Sean took a deep breath of the bracing air. And then he saw the figure standing in the shadows near the back wall. Startled, he started to dash back through the door and go for his gun.

"I guess you couldn't sleep either?"

His dad. "What are you doing out here?"

Troy stepped away from the wall. "Reliving the good times."

"Didn't the doctor tell you that you needed to get your rest?"

"Sometimes I rest better out here than anywhere else. Lots of nights when I couldn't sleep, I'd come out here to keep from waking your mother. She'd wake up, anyway, the first time she rolled over and I wasn't lying there beside her. Sometimes we'd dance in the moonlight. Mostly, she danced and I just held her until whatever problems that were keeping me awake seemed not to matter anymore."

"I don't need to hear this."

"I think maybe you do, Sean. You listened to your mother's family for years. You've heard exaggerated versions of all my shortcomings. You've heard how I was never good enough for Helene. You've heard how she planned to take you and your brothers and leave me. Now maybe it's time you heard my side of the story."

Sean dropped to the metal bench and propped his bare feet on a cold, hard stone. "Fair enough."

"Your mother was too good for me, Sean. She may have been too good for any mere mortal, but she was definitely too good for me."

Troy began to pace the narrow, meandering walkway. "She was upper crust. I made just enough money wrangling to pay the entry fee of every rodeo I could get to. But from the moment I met her, I knew that all I wanted was to love her and do my best to make her happy."

"So what went wrong?"

"Between us? Not a damn thing, except that it was a constant struggle to keep our heads about the poverty line. Your mother never complained, and she could stretch a dollar so far you'd swear it was made of rubber. She loved you boys and she loved me, and that was all she needed to make her happy. I know you were young, but you have to remember how happy we were back then."

The memories rained down on Sean with hurricane force. Laughing at Dakota's ridiculous knock-knock jokes. Taking turns jumping off Troy's shoulders at the swimming hole. Family nights when they watched movies together and had popcorn fights.

Happy was all he remembered until the happiness died.

"Why was Mother leaving you?"

"She was never leaving me. She was going to visit her parents, but she was never leaving me."

"But at the trial…"

"I know what some of the neighbors testified about your mother being afraid of me, or keeping secrets about me from her parents, Sean. All I can tell you is that if they were accurate, they were taking things out of context."

"Why would they?"

"Human nature, I guess. People got caught up in the heinous nature of the crime. The sheriff kept saying I was guilty and they started believing it. Not everyone, but enough that things just started snowballing against me.

"But it's my fault, too, Sean. I didn't fight for myself. I didn't care what happened to me. I couldn't stand it that I woke up in the mornings. I couldn't bear the thought of keeping on breathing and going through the motions of life when Helene would not be there with me. I just drowned in my own selfish grief."

The anguish in Troy's voice tore at Sean's soul. It was difficult not to believe he was telling the truth. The man's soul was tortured. But Sean had needed to hear this years ago. He'd needed a father. He'd needed something to hold on to when he was only thirteen and his world was disintegrating in his hands.

"I wanted to die back then, too," Sean admitted for the first time in his life. "I tried to kill myself. I just didn't have the guts to pull the trigger."

Troy walked over and stopped beside Sean, so close that their shadows mingled into one. "I let you down, son. I let all of you boys down. Helene may never forgive me for that. I'll never forgive myself, but for what it's worth, I'm sorrier than you can ever know."

"I'm sorry, too. I'm glad we had this talk. I just wish it had come seventeen years ago, when I so desperately needed my father."

"I can't change the past. But I'm here now. The rest is up to you."

Sean felt a clammy emptiness invade his soul as he walked away. He wished that a few words from his father could change things the way they'd done when he was a boy. He wished he could reach out to his father and say that all was forgiven and that they'd just start over and things would be fine between them.

But words couldn't reach his soul. He didn't even turn when he heard Troy walk back into the house and close the door behind him.

EVE WOKE UP AT SIX, a full hour before the alarm clock would go off. She slid out of bed, a little nervous, but still eager to start the day. She'd lain awake for hours last night before she'd finally made a decision.

Going to Dallas and putting herself in Detective Conner's hands was risky at best. Staying at the ranch, hoping Orson Bastion wouldn't track her down, was like waiting on a lit fuse to blow. Given enough time, he'd find her. When that happened, she knew that Sean would do everything in his power to protect her and Joey.

That might not be enough. And even if it was, Joey would still be exposed to the violence.

Sean had the only viable solution. Change continents. Bastion would never travel to Europe to chase her down. Even if he had the money and the will, he wouldn't risk flying on a fake passport. More than likely, he wouldn't even risk airport security to fly inside the states.

As far as falling for Sean, that was a moot point. She already loved him. Joey's attachment was the more difficult issue, but somehow they'd work it out.

Eve spent the next hour packing. She wouldn't take much—one suitcase for her and one for Joey, plus a small carry-on. If she forgot something they had to have, they could buy it in Italy.

By the time she finished, Joey was twisting and turning. He'd wake soon, so she'd have to hurry if she wanted to be dressed before he got up. Rushing to the guest bath just down the hall, she brushed her teeth, washed her face and dressed.

"Momma. Where are you?"

Eve added the usual touch of blush and lip gloss and went back to the bedroom to check on her son. She'd tell Sean her decision right after breakfast. She'd wait until the last minute to tell Joey, leaving him just enough time to tell the horses goodbye, and not enough time to get anxious before they were off on their adventure.

Italy with Sean, instead of Texas with Orson Bastion. She pinched herself hard to convince herself she wasn't dreaming. The only thing that proved she wasn't was that tiny shred of apprehension that wouldn't quite disappear.

"EVE, THIS IS COLLETTE. Have you seen the morning news?"

"No, we're just having breakfast. Sean made pancakes. You should come join us."

"Don't let anyone turn the TV on until I can get there to pick up Joey."

The urgency in Collette's voice sent rivers of fear coursing through Eve. She pushed her chair back from the table and walked to the family room so that she was out of hearing range of the others. "What's happened, Collette?"

"It's bad, Eve. Really bad. But wait until I get Joey out of there before you deal with it."

"Just tell me," Eve insisted. "I can handle it."

"There was an explosion last night."

"Where?"

"In Dallas."

"Does this have anything to do with Orson Bastion?"

"Please, Eve. Don't make me talk about it. I'll start crying, and it's best if Joey doesn't see me that upset."

Eve's stomach churned. "Has there been another terrorist attack?"

"No, nothing like that."

"Then get over here on the double."

"I'm on my way."

Eve picked up the remote, fighting the urge to flick on a local cable news channel and find out what kind of explosion had Collette this upset. Whatever it was, she refused to let it sabotage her plans. Nothing short of Orson's arrest could make her want to deal with the kind of frenzied terror she'd heard in Collette's voice.

Sean came to the door of the family room. "Was that Gordon on the phone?"

"No, it was Collette. She's on her way over to pick up Joey."

"Is that all? You look upset."

"Collette sounded near hysteria."

"About what?"

"She refused to say, except that it's about something she doesn't want me to see on the news channel until Joey is out of the house."

Sean's muscles clenched and the veins in his neck bulged into corded lines. "It's that son of a bitch Orson again. I'd love to get my hands on that bastard and show him what it feels like to be on the receiving end of misery."

And Eve prayed he'd never get close enough to Orson to get that chance. She wanted him to stay far away from Orson's sick brand of evil.

"I'll see if Troy feels up to taking Joey for a walk to the horse barn. If Collette's that upset, she'll only frighten Joey."

Eve nodded and tightened her grip on the remote. It seemed an eternity before she heard the back door slam shut.

"All clear," Sean said, as he joined her in the den. "Troy's got things under control."

Eve turned on the TV and read the rolling caption beneath the picture. An explosion in Dallas. Two police officers killed. And then she saw the image and she knew that Italy was officially off the table.

Chapter Fourteen

"A house explosion last night in a quiet Dallas neighborhood left two local police officers dead and the house in ruins. Neighbors as far as five blocks away reported being wakened by the blast. The owner of the house, Eve Worthington, was not at home when the explosion occurred. She has not been reached for comment, but we hope to have a statement from her soon."

The news went on and on. The words were like garbled static scratching across Eve's mind. She struggled to make sense of the continuous barrage of meaningless interviews with neighbors she barely knew and a police spokesperson who talked in circles, never zeroing in on the sordid truth.

A different reporter appeared on the screen. This one talked of Eve's connection to the prison system and mentioned that she'd

worked not only with recently escaped prisoner Orson Bastion, but with Troy Ledger.
Apparently, they'd done their homework.

The reporter further mentioned that Eve
had recommended against Orson's parole and
that she'd gone on record as saying that she
would trust convicted wife-killer Troy Ledger
with her life.

The screen divided into two sections. The
reporter on the right reminded the viewing
audience that it was Eve's husband who was
killed in a drive-by shooting in that same
neighborhood almost two years ago. She questioned if the two events could be related.

The screen switched back to a view of Eve's
house—or rather its charred remains. This
time the view was much clearer. The chim-
ney stood like a lone general whose soldiers
had died in the flames. Part of a huge beam
lay over the untouched brick mailbox at the
street.

Joey's room was gone completely. All his
favorite possessions had turned to ashes. All
the things he should have gone home to when
this nightmare was over were destroyed. Even
the bed he would have been sleeping in if
she'd stayed in Dallas had apparently become

incendiary fuel for the blaze that had claimed their home.

Her stomach rolled.

She jumped up and ran to the bathroom, making it there just in time to throw up what felt like the lining of her stomach. Sean wet a cloth with cold water and held it to her head. She hated he was seeing her this way.

"There's no need to hear more," he said.

Tears burned in her eyes. "I've lost everything. Joey's baby book. My pictures. Letters from my mother before she died of cancer. My father's dog tags and the flag from the top of his coffin. It's all gone."

"Maybe not. You know how news reporters are. They always show things from the worst possible angle. Some of the treasures may be salvageable."

"The house is gone, Sean. There is no good angle. I should have known Orson would win."

"He didn't win. You're alive, Eve, and so is Joey."

"But how many other people will have to die before he stops seeking his demonic revenge?"

Sean tried to pull her into his arms, but the emotional trauma wouldn't let her accept comfort. She beat her fists into his chest. "How many others? And how long before he finds a way to get to me?"

"He'll never get to you. I won't let him."

"You can't stop him. Can't you see that? No one can."

"I can stop him," Sean said. "And I will."

But he couldn't; and if he tried he'd end up dead. They might all end up dead. The next explosion could be here in this house, with them inside it.

Tears poured down her cheeks and shudders shook her body. This time, when Sean took her in his arms, she held on tight and kept holding on until she ran out of tears.

There was only one sane thing left for her to do, and it did not involve a trip to Italy.

THE FIRE HAD BEEN A SIGHT to behold. Eve's house had become a glorious inferno that lit the sky in brilliant shades of reds, oranges and yellows. Orson had been close enough to feel the heat and to hear the crackle and pop as the support beams fell and the wood splintered.

It had been quite a night, one that he hadn't spent in the mold-infested, mildewed cabin on Lake Livingston. This grimy motel room wasn't much better, but it was only for a night.

All that was left was for him to pick up the money from Alyssa and kidnap Nick.

Then look out, Mexico. Escaped convict Orson Bastion was headed to a bar near you.

Orson loaded his toothbrush with a minty paste and turned on the TV so that he could bask in his success while he brushed his full three minutes. He surfed three stations till he hit pay dirt. Ah, yes. They were even giving him credit for his handiwork. He walked back to the bathroom to spit.

When he returned, the reporter was talking about Troy Ledger and contrasting what Eve had said about him at the time of his release on a technicality, to what she'd testified at Orson's parole hearing.

She'd trust Troy Ledger with her life. Like the man could—

Orson choked on the toothpaste when the truth practically pounced from the TV and into his mind.

Eve had run to Troy Ledger when she'd heard that Orson had escaped prison. He'd saved her life once, so she assumed he could do it again.

Now they were talking about Troy's ranch in Mustang Run. This was priceless. There would be a slight delay in reaching Mexico while Orson devised a new strategy.

He could make good on his threat and avenge his mother's death. He owed that to Lydia and to himself.

"Oh, no. Not again. This is exactly how it was the day Troy returned from prison."

Eve rushed to the front window and peeked over Collette's shoulder to see what she was talking about.

"It's the media sharks," Collette said. "They go on a feeding frenzy anytime they smell a story that involves the infamous Troy Ledger."

Eve stared, horrified at the crowds gathering not ten yards from the front door. "This is private property. They can't just drive onto this land."

"They can unless someone stops them."

"The sheriff should."

"My dad's the sheriff," Collette said. "He'd come and bring his deputies if Troy called him, but Troy won't. There's a bit of bad blood between them. It goes way back and is much too complicated to get into today."

Sean and Dylan strode into the room

together. "Don't gawk at them," Sean said. "It will only encourage them to start popping flashbulbs."

When two more vans drove up, Eve said, "You should call the sheriff and have those people arrested for trespassing."

"I'm way ahead of you. Dylan and I have already hired an Austin security firm to disperse this crowd as peacefully as possible, and to stand guard at the gate to keep others from getting in."

"There will be some who'll just bust through the fence and tear up the pastures to try and get the scoop," Dylan said. "But we'll have guards around the house twenty-four seven."

"Then you expected this?" Eve asked.

"From the second you turned on the TV this morning." Sean put a hand on Eve's shoulder. "And don't start blaming yourself. You're the victim, not the aggressor."

But she was the one who'd brought this on the Ledgers—and while Troy was still recovering from a coronary attack.

"Has anyone seen Joey?" Eve asked, fighting panic when she didn't hear his miniature cars rolling up and down the hallway.

"He's watching Dad shave," Dylan said.

"Dad's trying to convince him that it doesn't hurt when the hairs come off."

"He's not used to having a man in the house," Eve said.

"Okay, here's the new and approved house rules," Sean announced. "No female leaves this house without a male accompanying her. And by male, I mean an adult male, not Joey."

"Isn't that going a bit overboard?" Collette questioned. "The media mongrels may hound and aggravate us, but they're not actually dangerous."

"It's not the press they're concerned about," Eve said. "It's Orson Bastion. With this many reporters checking out everything in sight, it's only a matter of time until one of them reports that I'm here."

"I hadn't thought of that." Collette went back to the window, pushed back the curtain and looked out. "Your car's gone, Eve."

"I moved it into the large shed behind the house," Sean said. "It's no longer in the open, but someone will snoop around and get the license plate number. I moved the packages and the rest of your luggage that was in the trunk into the garden bedroom, Eve, in case you need them."

"Thanks." What she had with her now was all she had.

Joey came running down the hallway. "Guess what?"

"The circus is coming to town," Sean muttered under his breath.

Beside him, Eve whispered, "I'm pretty sure it's already here."

Joey asked his question again.

"Tell us." Sean moved to the window and closed the shutter, blocking out the sunshine along with the crowd.

Joey obliged, eager to share his news. "Mr. Ledger said we can decorate the tree today, and not with that old stuff you buy at the store. We're making our own decorations, and guess what else?"

Sean put his fingers to his temple as if her were concentrating. "We're going to string popcorn for the tree, and we can eat all we want."

Joey kicked the air. "How did you know?"

"I have super, bionic brain cells."

"And he did the same thing when he was a kid," Troy said.

Eve knew they were keeping this light for Joey's sake. She loved them for it, but it didn't change what she had to do. But first she'd decorate that tree and let Joey add his own special Christmas favorites. Then hopefully, she'd find a private moment to kiss Sean one last time before she took matters in her own hands. Well, hers and Detective Conner's.

ALYSSA'S HEART FLOPPED AROUND in her chest like a dying goldfish when the TV talked about Eve Worthington and her son. The boy was not even six years old yet, and he'd already seen his father shot down in cold blood. Now his house had burned to the ground.

They kept talking about Orson knowing the woman and how she was the shrink who said that if he got paroled, he'd kill someone else. Eve Worthington didn't know the half of it. Now that their mother had died, no one knew the truth about Orson and what he was capable of except Alyssa.

She had no doubts but that he'd blown up that shrink's house. He'd known how to make bombs since high school. He'd downloaded directions from the internet. Orson always said he could learn everything he needed to know from the internet. Everyone could, if they knew how to look for it.

But Orson wouldn't be satisfied with just blowing up that woman's house, not after what

she did to him. Alyssa knew Orson was hanging around Texas for a reason. And it wasn't
just the cash he'd had her get. If it had been,
he'd have picked up the money yesterday.

He was going to kill that woman, and then
her son would have nobody.

Alyssa had covered for Orson all his life.
First it had been because her mother had made
her. Now it was because she was afraid of
him.

But killing a kid's mother just wasn't right.

Alyssa stuck her hand in her pocket and
pulled out the card Detective Reagan Conner
had given her. She had the money and the
time and the godforsaken place to meet Orson
so that she could turn over his escape funds.

She punched in the number and waited.

"Conner speaking."

"Detective, this is Alyssa Coleman."

"I was hoping we'd hear from you. Do you
have information that will help us locate you
brother?"

"Yes sir, I do."

BY FOUR IN THE AFTERNOON, all was quiet
on the Ledger lawn. But even more disturbing for Eve than the hordes of noisy reporters

were the armed guards who were being paid to keep the media and Orson Bastion away.

Joey in his innocence had said it best. "Momma, make those men go home."

She was about to do just that.

Eve ran her fingers along the back of the ornate wooden garden bench and listened to the soothing sounds of water trickling into the fountain just in front of her. The garden was just one of the things she'd miss about the ranch. Mostly, she'd miss Sean.

With luck she'd be back in a few days to pick up Joey, but she knew in her heart that things between her and Sean would never be the same once she left the ranch.

Dropping to the bench, she opened her notebook and began to write.

Dear Sean,
I know I'm a coward for not saying this in person, but it would only start an argument that I'm not willing to lose. I came here looking for a place to hide. I found that and so much more. You were great with Joey and you taught this stubborn psychiatrist who thought she knew it all a lot about boys—and about cowboys. All good, I might add.

So now I need to ask you a huge favor. Please watch over Joey for me until I can return for him. Hopefully, that will be in a few days, but it won't be until Orson Bastion is either dead or back behind bars. I've brought too much chaos and danger to the Willow Creek Ranch already. And I don't want Orson Bastion anywhere near my son.

FYI. When this is over, I'll be available for dinner on the Grand Canal. Or in a dimly lit bistro in Paris, Texas. Your call.
Ciao,
Eve

That should do it. Not too heavy. Not too light. And hopefully, the part about dinner wasn't too pathetic.

She sealed the envelope and dropped it in her pocket.

Taking out her phone, she punched in the number for Detective Conner.

"Conner here.

"This is Eve Worthington."

"I'm guessing your call means that you caught the morning news."

"The news that the two officers you would

have used to protect me blew up with my house? Yeah, I heard."

"I would have had more than two on the scene if you'd been in the house."

"So you've said."

"I promised to protect you if you returned to Dallas. That promise still holds."

"So, do you have any other suggestions on how to use me as bait?"

"Look, Miss Worthington. It's been a rough night. I'm sorry about your house. Real sorry. I'm even sorrier that two young police officers lost their lives. And I'm plenty pissed off that we let Orson Bastion get away. So do me a favor and cut the sarcasm."

"I wasn't trying to be sarcastic, just realistic. I was also wondering why you didn't follow up on the money exchange between Orson and his sister."

"I can't discuss details concerning an ongoing case."

"Then can you discuss meeting me somewhere to figure out how I can help you flush out Orson?"

"I can arrange that. Why are you suddenly interested?"

"When Orson blew up my house, he also blew my cover. Soon, anyone who's interested will know that I'm staying at Troy Ledger's ranch in Mustang Run."

"Mustang Run is out of my jurisdiction. I can't promise any kind of protection unless you return to Dallas."

"Then let's make a deal."

"You sound as if you have terms."

"I do. Find a way to get me on every radio and TV station in the area. I want everyone to see that I'm back in Dallas. Leak where I'll be staying to the media, and then have enough men there to make sure you capture Orson Bastion while I'm still alive to celebrate."

"I can do that. I can also have a Texas Ranger pick you up at the Ledger ranch."

"That won't work. How about having him pick me up in Mustang Run? There's a big Baptist church on the highway, just after you pass the city limits sign. I'll be waiting in the parking lot in a black Honda."

"License plate number?"

She supplied it.

"I can have a ranger there in thirty minutes."

"I'll be waiting."

She went back inside just long enough to push the note under Sean's bedroom door. Then she went back to the garden and pushed the bench up against the stone wall that served as the back enclosure for the garden.

In seconds, she'd lifted herself to the top of the wall and jumped off on the other side. Her right ankle made an awkward landing. It smarted like crazy when she made a dash for her car.

Going though guards at the gate could present a problem, so she took Dylan's complaints about determined reporters at face value. She sped across the pasture, tearing down a couple of fences as she went, and doing major damage to her car's paint job.

When she reached the highway, she turned right.

That's when the doubts dragged her back into the confusing mire. What if she was making a major mistake? What if the detective couldn't protect her? What if she never saw Sean again?

What if Orson killed her as he had the others, and she missed out on the rest of Joey's life?

She tightened her grip on the wheel. What if this was the best option she had? Her gut feeling told her that it was. And at least, this way she could keep the danger far away from Joey.

Chapter Fifteen

"There's been a change in plans."

"What kind of change?"

The best kind, where Orson got to take care of things the right way. And since it was Saturday, Orson hadn't even had to work around Nick's school schedule. As he'd suspected, the kid was at the park most of the day.

"As you know, I didn't get a chance to pick up the money yesterday."

"Because you were too busy blowing up houses."

"You're getting a mouth on you, Alyssa. Mom wouldn't like it."

"Eve Worthington has a five-year-old son, Orson."

"I didn't tell her to have him."

"But she did, and he needs her. You've done enough damage to her, Orson. You don't need to kill her."

"Are you forgetting what she did to Mother?"

"Mother took her own life. That was not Eve Worthington's doing."

"Mother died because that snooty, pseudo-psychiatrist caused me to be denied early parole. Now she has to pay."

"Please don't kill her, Orson. Just this once, have a little sympathy for someone besides yourself."

"You sound so sweet and caring. Too bad that doesn't work on me. I'll kill her and leave her for Troy Ledger to find at his favorite little fishing hole. He can fish her right out of the river."

"Then I'm through helping and covering for you, Orson. Don't come to me for anything ever again."

"Don't be foolish. Drop the money off exactly as I explained to you. Mistakes will not be tolerated."

"I won't do it, Orson, not if you kill that woman."

"I think you will." He reached over and yanked the gag out of Nick's mouth. "Say hello to your mother, Nick. She's having a very bad day at work."

THE GUARDS AT THE GATE were a nice touch. Perhaps Orson had underestimated Troy Ledger. But he wasn't particularly disturbed by the unexpected militia. He appreciated modifications that challenged his intellect.

He'd acquired and studied an online survey of the ranch that Ledger's in-laws had ordered several years back. As a result, Orson knew exactly where Dowman River dissected Ledger's spread and created the fishing hole Ledger had gone on about with the other fishermen types in prison.

And if Orson remembered correctly, if he turned onto Willow Creek Ranch just south of the Dowman-Lagoste Bridge, he could drive all the way to the ranch house without having to cross Willow Creek.

He made the turn and slowed, getting his bearings. A black Honda came up behind him and rode his tail. Not that it could legally pass him on this curving road. Orson checked out the driver in the rearview mirror.

A female, and on a practically deserted country road. She looked familiar. When she put on her blinker to pass, Orson pressed the accelerator. Once they hit the next curve, he slowed again.

She was familiar all right. That was Eve

Worthington. He smiled and slapped the back of the seat. "Too bad you can't see what we're about to do, Nick. This is going to be fun."

EVE HONKED AT THE IDIOT in front of her and raised an angry fist. He knew she wanted to pass him, but every time she got the chance, he'd speed up.

Finally, they hit a straight section of blacktop and he let her go around him. She pushed the speed limit, trying to make up for time she'd lost fooling around with that imbecile.

He sped up as well. He was riding her tail, too close for comfort. She slowed for him to pass her. Being late to the Baptist church in Mustang Run was better than getting killed in the car.

The driver came up even with her and then bumped her from the side. Her car shimmied but stayed on the pavement. Irritation turned to apprehension. This guy was playing dangerous.

He sideswiped her again, this time so hard the car skidded onto the shoulder. She guided the vehicle back onto the road, then slowed to a near stop, praying he'd just drive off and cease his deadly intimidation.

There was a bridge just ahead, and if he ran

her off the road there, she'd be battered by the iron side rail. Both cars might plunge into Dowman River. One or both of them could get killed.

But the driver didn't wait for the bridge. He hammered his car into her back fender, knocking her sideways. She struggled to keep control of the car, but it skidded across the narrow road and went flying down an embankment.

When it finally came to rest, her car was practically lying on its right side. Her head seem to be spinning in dizzying circles. When she could finally focus, she got her first good look at the man who'd run her off the road.

Orson Bastion was only steps away.

Somehow Eve managed to unbuckle the seat belt and get the driver's side door open. She took off running for the woods, but before she made it out of the clearing, Orson's strong hands grabbed her from behind and threw her to the ground.

He planted his foot on her neck and pointed a pistol at her head.

"Take it easy and I won't kill you. Not here, anyway, and certainly not with the pleasant, quick death a bullet to the brain would provide.

"I have something much more torturous in mind for you. And then I will leave your body for Troy to find. Now, won't that be an exciting conclusion to the drama in our minds?"

SEAN HAD WANDERED all through the house twice, looking for Eve. He'd found Collette and Joey playing checkers in one of the spare bedrooms. Neither had seen Eve.

Sean stopped when he got to his own bedroom and stuck his head inside. No sign of Eve, but there was an unopened envelope on the floor, addressed to him. He picked it up and turned it over in his hand a few times, as if he could figure out who it was from by feel.

Finally, he slipped his thumb beneath the seal and tore the envelope open. He checked out the name at the bottom first.

Eve.

Apprehension sent him on yet another adrenaline high. There was no way a note from Eve could be good, especially when she was nowhere to be found.

Sean dropped to the side of the bed and read every word—twice—trying to make sense of why Eve would try a fool stunt like this.

Why go to Conner for protection when

Sean was doing everything he knew to do to keep her safe? He had security guards at the gate, security outside the house, plus the three Ledger men.

Feeling positively betrayed, he took the note to Troy. "You know her," he said, once Troy had skimmed the note. "What do you make of this?"

"It's pretty clear that what she's asking is for you to take care of Joey while she goes to Dallas."

"I offer protection and she chooses the police. If you were me, what would you do in my situation?"

"I'd ask Dylan and me to stay here and protect Joey and Collette, while I went to Dallas and made sure Orson did not get his hands on my woman."

Sean was thinking the exact thing, not that Eve was acting much like she was his woman.

Not that he'd ever asked her to be.

Troy's cell phone jangled.

"Maybe that's Eve calling to say she's come to her senses," Sean said.

Troy took the call and shifted it to speakerphone.

"Hello."

"This is Detective Reagan Conner. Eve Worthington was supposed to meet a Texas Ranger at the Baptist Church in Mustang Run about ten minutes ago. She never showed up. I was wondering if you knew anything about that."

"Maybe she's changed her mind and is heading back here," Sean said, responding for Troy.

"That could be, but we received a phone call from an anonymous tipster a few minutes ago. She said that Orson was either at or heading to the Willow Creek Ranch right now. She said he plans to kill Eve and leave her body at Troy Ledger's favorite fishing hole."

Sean uttered a stream of curses.

"We're on it," Troy said. "How about sending that ranger down to the Dowman-Lagoste Bridge. And tell him to be on the lookout for Orson Bastion."

Troy killed the connection.

"The only fishing hole of mine that Bastion could possibly know about is the one just south of the bridge," Troy said.

"I know right where that is. Call Dylan. Tell him I may need backup. You and the guards stay here with Joey and Collette, in case Bastion doubles back here."

Sean raced out the back door without waiting for agreement. He could cover the distance a lot faster by horseback than by winding roads. And there was no time to waste.

EVE WATCHED ORSON'S MOVEMENTS, though she could do nothing to alter them. She was tied to a downed tree trunk with only her feet and hands free. He was busily tying lengths of rope around her ankles.

"Have you ever watched someone drown, Eve? It's a mesmerizing sight. They gasp for breath and fling their arms as if they've just jumped off a building and are trying to fly. Then everything just goes limp. They exhale bubbles like bizarre-shaped fish."

"You drowned that boy when you were twelve, didn't you, Orson? You killed him just to watch him die."

"My, you do surprise me. I'm sure you didn't discover that when you were digging around in my head. You were never good at that, you know."

"I learned enough about you to recognize that you're a psychopath." She had to keep him talking. The longer he talked the longer she'd stay alive, and the better her chances to be rescued, though Sean would never come looking for her after reading that note.

Still, she needed to keep Orson talking.

"You overdosed your girlfriend, too, didn't you? How did that go? Did you persuade her to take the drugs on her own, or did you just crush the pills and shoot them directly into her veins?"

Orson removed some three-holed bricks from a canvas bag and laid them at his feet. Then he picked up one and began to weave the rope that bound her right foot through the holes.

"I administered them through the veins. She was hardly worth persuasion. She'd slept with half my friends and then swore to me that she hadn't."

He picked up the next brick and began the rope weaving again. "That boy you asked about deserved to drown, too. He called my mother a whore."

"Was she?"

"Don't talk about my mother. You killed her. Isn't that enough?"

"Your mother committed suicide."

"Because you lied to keep me in jail forever. You had no idea what I was capable of. You're the reason Brock had to die, too."

"But now you're going to kill my son's mother. Isn't that just as wrong?"

"You should have thought about that before you ruined my life."

He held up one of her feet. The three bricks he'd weaved into the rope made the foot feel as if it was carved from granite.

"Time to go sleep with the fishes. And then your buddy Troy Ledger can come and catch you one day." He chuckled as he bound her wrists tightly and then untied her from the log. Circling a burly arm beneath her shoulders, he dragged her toward the water.

"Don't do this, Orson. Let me go free and I'll tell the parole board that I was wrong. I'll tell them anything you want."

"It's rather late for that. I no longer care what the parole board does, and I never will again. If I went back to prison now, they'd make sure that I died there. But it doesn't matter. I won't be going back."

He shoved her into the water and the icy depth swirled around her waist and then up to her shoulders.

"Not quite deep enough yet," he taunted, "but don't worry. The end will come soon enough."

Weighed down by the heavy bricks, her feet began to sink into the mud. A few more inches and she wouldn't be able to keep her mouth and nose above water.

She would die here, just the way Orson had described the other drowning—flinging her arms the way she was now, wild but unsuccessful, with her wrists bound tightly. She'd struggle to keep her head above water, but none of that would save her.

The surface of the water reached her neck and sprayed over her chin. She thought of Sean and the way he smiled and tipped his hat. He was all man all the time. Yet he'd been so good with Joey. She'd worried that Sean wasn't a forever kind of guy. Now it turned out her forever might be measured in minutes.

She screamed for help at the top of her lungs.

She didn't want to die. She wanted to raise her son. She was all he had. She loved him so very, very much.

Water splashed into her mouth. Her movements became frantic as she fought to keep her head above water.

She screamed again.

She did not want to die.

But the mud was well over her ankles now and the thick, gooey mass just kept sucking her in.

Chapter Sixteen

The stallion's hooves flew across the uneven ground and through the carpet of brown leaves and high grass. Sean urged him faster still. He'd never get over it if something terrible happened to Eve.

He shouldn't have let her out of his sight. He knew how fearful she was of Orson, yet how protective she was of Joey.

A piecing scream reverberated through the trees. It was Eve. Orson must have her and be doing sickening, terrifying things to her.

Sean would kill him if he hurt Eve. He would. He'd kill him and be as heartless about it as Orson was with his crimes.

He urged his mount on. "Come through for me, Gunner. Come through for me this time and I promise you'll never become glue."

The scream sounded again. It was closer this time. Sean knew he had to be getting close to the bridge, and the old fishing hole was only another hundred yards or so downstream from there.

The evening was too quiet now. Sean longed for another scream, any sound to let him know that Eve was still alive.

Something rustled in the woods to Sean's left. He readied his rifle but kept galloping. The next sound he recognized instantly. It was the gentle lap of water against the riverbank. And just off to the north he spotted the bridge.

He turned south, traveling along the river's edge until he spotted a car next to the treeline. He scanned the area, his finger poised on the trigger of his firearm.

No one was in sight. He slid from the horse's back and led the animal toward the car, alert for anyone hiding in the trees or jumping from inside or behind the vehicle.

Something splashed in the water, capturing all his attention. A head was bobbing frantically, barely staying above the surface. Sean dropped the reins and took off at a dead run.

It was Eve. Fighting for her life. His heart beat wildly, slamming against his chest as he dropped his rifle and jumped into the water, boots and all.

"Don't waste the effort."

Neck deep and dripping, Sean turned to see Orson Bastion standing on the bank with a pistol pointed at Sean's head.

"Kill me, but not Eve," Sean pleaded. "Let her go home and raise her son." He was feet from her, and her frantic gasps filled him with determination. He'd die to save her. He had no choice.

But his plea had no effect on Bastion. "Sorry. It's goodbye cruel world for both of you."

Before Sean could even make a last desperate grab for Eve, the sound of gunfire thundered across the water. He steeled himself for searing pain, or worse, the sight of Eve's beautiful face covered in blood. But it never came.

He grabbed for Eve, slipping his arm under her chin so that he could keep her from sliding beneath the water. "I've got you," he told her. Then he looked back toward the shore for Orson. He hadn't been prepared for the scene in front of him.

Orson was lying on the ground and Troy was standing over him, gun in hand.

"Need any help?" Troy called, not taking his eyes off the monster.

For Sean, relief had never felt so good. He finally remembered to breathe again. "A ride home in a warm car would be nice."

Struggling with the weight of the bricks, he dragged Eve to the shore. She took in huge gulps of air and tried to speak, but fear and the frigid water kept her chattering. "Th-thank y-you. Sean, I—I—"

He silenced her and carried her to the river-bank. She'd have plenty of time to thank him later. Plenty of time for him to tell her how his life had almost ended with hers.

Troy took off his jacket and threw it over her shoulders, and then he slit the ropes that bound her wrists and ankles.

Though she was safe now, Sean could not bring himself to let her out of his arms for even a second, but he leaned over for a glimpse at Orson. "Is he dead?"

"Probably," Troy replied, "but I'll call an ambulance just in case he isn't. And the ranger should be showing up here any second. Now you two best get in my car and start the heater. It's parked just on the other side of that hill."

"What happed to Dylan?" Sean asked, as

he made sure Eve could walk to the car. "I thought you were sending him as backup."

"He's at home protecting the woman and Joey. I figured it's a father's privilege to come to the aid of his son."

He stopped and turned to look at Troy. "If you hadn't arrived when you did, we'd both be dead."

"'Bout time I did something right."

"You're always right in my book," Eve murmured through chattering teeth. "But thanks again."

"Yeah." Sean put one arm around Troy's shoulder. "Thanks, *Dad*."

The emotion was genuine, and surprisingly, saying "Dad" out loud didn't feel half bad.

Epilogue

The presents had all been opened. Joey was on the floor with the golden retriever puppy Troy had given him for Christmas, after making sure it was all right with Eve. Eve had never seen her son so happy.

Collette wound the bright blue scarf around her neck. "I love this color, Eve. You give the neatest gifts. I should start taking you with me every time I go shopping for clothes."

"Sales start next week. And Troy, thanks for the gift certificate," Eve said. "I'm going to go out and replace some of what I lost in the fire."

The celebration continued, but Eve slipped away and walked out to Helene's garden. The pots of poinsettias Collette had scattered throughout the beds gave the whole space a festive look. It was lost on Eve.

She hadn't told anyone yet that this was her

and Joey's last day on the ranch. It was time to move on. Orson had survived, but he was back behind bars where he'd no doubt stay. His nephew Nick was safe and back with his mother. Eve would get her insurance settlement from the house fire soon. And she'd found a house to rent, one with a fenced yard that was big enough for Joey's dog.

And while Sean still seemed absolutely crazy about her, he hadn't mentioned the possibility of a future together. She shouldn't be surprised. He was a fabulous lover, a brave protector, a genuine horseman and cowboy. But he was not a forever kind of guy.

Tears burned in the back of Eve's eyes as she dropped to the bench. She loved Sean, and she doubted she'd ever stop missing him. But she couldn't change who he was, and it wouldn't be fair to try.

"Eve."

She turned and saw Sean step out into the courtyard.

"You left before you opened all your gifts and before I told you my news."

Eve blinked repeatedly, determined to hold back the tears. "What is your news?"

"I put a down payment on some acreage

near Bandera. I've decided to breed and train quarter horses."

So he had made his plans without discussing them with her. That pretty much said it all.

"If that's what you want, I'm happy for you."

"That's not quite all of it. I want to run a program where I bring out troubled kids on the weekends and let them ride and help with the horses. I know I won't reach all of them, but I think I can make a difference with some."

"You'll be great at that," she said honestly.

"Now, about the gift that you didn't open."

A tear escaped and she turned away from him. "I need to check on Joey. I'll open the gift later." She started past him, but he grabbed her arm and turned her around.

"Joey's fine. The gift can't wait."

He slid his hand down her arm and took her hand in his. Then he dropped to one knee. "I love you, Eve. I love Joey, too. Marry me so that we can be a real family. I need the horses, but we can have a place in town, too, if you want."

"The ranch is not a problem. I'd love living on a ranch. So would Joey."

"Then say you'll marry me."

She ached to say yes, but there was one question that needed answering. "Are you going to leave me standing at the altar?"

"Not a chance."

"How can you be so sure?"

"Because I was wrong about not being a forever kind of guy. I just hadn't met the right woman to share forever with."

"Are you sure?"

"Very sure. And if you don't say yes fast, I'm going to go crazy."

Her heart felt so full that it might burst from her chest. "In that case, I love you with all my heart, Sean Ledger, and yes, I'll marry you. I will so marry you."

He rose to his feet and touched his lips to hers with a kiss that promised a million golden tomorrows.

"I can't wait to start our new life together," Sean said. "Now let's go tell Dad that he's not losing a puppy, he's gaining a grandson."

* * * * *

LARGER-PRINT BOOKS!

GET 2 FREE LARGER-PRINT NOVELS

PLUS 2 FREE GIFTS!

HARLEQUIN®

INTRIGUE®

Breathtaking Romantic Suspense

YES! Please send me 2 FREE LARGER-PRINT Harlequin Intrigue® novels and my 2 FREE gifts (gifts are worth about $10). After receiving them, if I don't wish to receive any more books, I can return the shipping statement marked "cancel." If I don't cancel, I will receive 6 brand-new novels every month and be billed just $4.99 per book in the U.S. or $5.74 per book in Canada. That's a saving of at least 13% off the cover price! It's quite a bargain! Shipping and handling is just 50¢ per book.* I understand that accepting the 2 free books and gifts places me under no obligation to buy anything. I can always return a shipment and cancel at any time. Even if I never buy another book from Harlequin, the two free books and gifts are mine to keep forever.

199/399 HDN E5MS

Name _____ (PLEASE PRINT)

Address _____ Apt. #

City _____ State/Prov. _____ Zip/Postal Code

Signature (if under 18, a parent or guardian must sign)

Mail to the **Harlequin Reader Service:**
IN U.S.A.: P.O. Box 1867, Buffalo, NY 14240-1867
IN CANADA: P.O. Box 609, Fort Erie, Ontario L2A 5X3
Not valid for current subscribers to Harlequin Intrigue Larger-Print books.

Are you a subscriber to Harlequin Intrigue books and want to receive the larger-print edition? Call 1-800-873-8635 today!

* Terms and prices subject to change without notice. Prices do not include applicable taxes. N.Y. residents add applicable sales tax. Canadian residents will be charged applicable provincial taxes and GST. Offer not valid in Quebec. This offer is limited to one order per household. All orders subject to approval. Credit or debit balances in a customer's account(s) may be offset by any other outstanding balance owed by or to the customer. Please allow 4 to 6 weeks for delivery. Offer available while quantities last.

Your Privacy: Harlequin Books is committed to protecting your privacy. Our Privacy Policy is available online at www.eHarlequin.com or upon request from the Reader Service. From time to time we make our lists of customers available to reputable third parties who may have a product or service of interest to you. If you would prefer we not share your name and address, please check here. ☐

Help us get it right—We strive for accurate, respectful and relevant communications. To clarify or modify your communication preferences, visit us at www.ReaderService.com/consumerchoice.

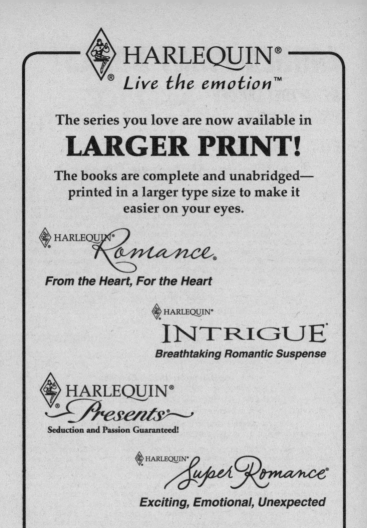